Ally Blake

A NIGHT WITH THE
SOCIETY PLAYBOY

NIGHTS *of* PASSION

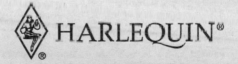

HARLEQUIN®

TORONTO • NEW YORK • LONDON
AMSTERDAM • PARIS • SYDNEY • HAMBURG
STOCKHOLM • ATHENS • TOKYO • MILAN • MADRID
PRAGUE • WARSAW • BUDAPEST • AUCKLAND

ISBN-13: 978-0-373-12778-8
ISBN-10:   0-373-12778-2

A NIGHT WITH THE SOCIETY PLAYBOY

First North American Publication 2008.

www.eHarlequin.com

Printed in U.S.A.

Welcome to the November 2008 collection of Harlequin Presents! What better way to warm up in the coming winter months than with a hot novel from your favorite Presents author—and this month we have plenty in-store to keep you cozy! Don't miss *Ruthlessly Bedded by the Italian Billionaire* by Emma Darcy, in which a case of mistaken identity leads Jenny Kent to a billionaire's bed. Plus, be sure to look out for *The Sheikh's Wayward Wife*, the second installment of Sandra Marton's fantastic trilogy THE SHEIKH TYCOONS, and Robyn Donald's final story in her brilliant MEDITERRANEAN PRINCES duet, *The Mediterranean Prince's Captive Virgin*.

Also this month, read the story of sexy Italian Joe Mendez and single mom Rachel in *Mendez's Mistress* by favorite author Anne Mather. And in Kate Walker's *Bedded by the Greek Billionaire*, a gorgeous Greek seeks revenge on an English rose—by making her his mistress! Vincenzo is intent on claiming his son from estranged wife Emma in *Sicilian Husband, Unexpected Baby* by Sharon Kendrick, while Susan Napier brings you *Public Scandal, Private Mistress*, in which unsuspecting Veronica becomes involved with billionaire Luc. Finally, in Ally Blake's *A Night with the Society Playboy*, Caleb wants just one more night with the woman who walked out on him ten years ago....

We'd love to hear what you think about Presents. E-mail us at Presents@hmb.co.uk or join in the discussions at www.iheartpresents.com and www.sensationalromance.blogspot.com, where you'll also find more information about books and authors!

What do you look for in a guy?
Charisma. Sex appeal. Confidence. A body
to die for. Looks that stand out from the crowd.
Well, look no further—the heroes in this
miniseries have all of this, and more! And now
that they've met the women in these novels,
there is one thing on everyone's mind....

One night is never enough!

These guys know what they want and how
they're going to get it!

All about the author...
Ally Blake

When **ALLY BLAKE** was a little girl, she made a wish that when she turned twenty-six she would marry an Italian two years older than herself. After it actually came true, she realized she was onto something with these wish things. So, next she wished that she could make a living spending her days in her pajamas, eating M&Ms and drinking scads of coffee while using her formative experiences of wallowing in teenage crushes and romantic movies to create love stories of her own.

The fact that she is now able to spend her spare time searching the Internet for pictures of handsome guys for research purposes is merely a bonus! Come along and visit her Web site at www.allyblake.com.

To my urban family, Chris Sheree,
Tom and Ben Breasley: the ones
who have made my time away from home
feel like home.

CHAPTER ONE

'WILL you, Damien Halliburton, take Chelsea London to be your lawful wedded wife?'

The minister's words blurred into one long onerous drone as Caleb, acting as best man to his mate and business partner, fidgeted inside his tux, stifled a yawn, and pretended as best he could to pay attention.

'I do,' Damien said, his voice deep and true, his eyes all for his admittedly scrumptious new bride.

Though he couldn't deny that Damien had seemed happier since Chelsea appeared on the scene, Caleb had long since decided that that kind of indiscriminate happiness was for chumps. Not only was it fleeting, once gone it invariably took a little piece of you with it.

And Caleb liked himself and all his pieces. Quite a bit in fact.

He enjoyed his privileged life. He adored the pursuits that came with it. tennis, sailing, golf, drinks at the club. The capacity to spend the occasional weekend basking on a private beach somewhere didn't go astray.

And he thrived on his work. He took great pleasure in doing whatever it took to land ostensibly ungettable clients for Keppler, Jones and Morgenstern day traders. Others in the biz thought him ruthless in his tunnel-visioned pursuit of the big fish. But the simple fact was he'd always found it too easy to make people say yes.

He'd been told by a former weekend getaway companion it had everything to do with a distracting glint in his eyes. It blinded people to the fact that he never switched off, he was always, always silently working out a way to come out on top.

To her credit it had taken him several seconds to realise she hadn't meant it as a compliment, or in fact a come-on, and by that stage she'd walked out his door never to darken it again.

Caleb glanced across the altar and caught the eye of Kensey, a bridesmaid, who also happened to be Chelsea's older sister. She was dark where Chelsea was fair, and he had always preferred brunettes.

He glinted for all he was worth.

Kensey's eyes grew wide before she flipped her left ring finger at him from beneath her bouquet. A gold wedding band flashed his way.

His smile only widened as he offered a shrug by way of apology, but as he moved his gaze away the smile twisted into a grimace. Was the whole damn world getting married?

He gave himself a mental pat on the back for deciding not to bring a date to this thing. Weddings stirred up all sorts of irrational emotions in people. He'd seen it before. Perfectly level-headed gents cut down by a giddy mix of floral scents, blinding amounts of pink satin, and over-indulgence in cake frosting.

Finding that scrunching his toes in his shoes wasn't proving distracting enough to keep him from yawning again, Caleb looked over the extensive crowd that filled the elegant city church.

He called upon his well-tuned affluence radar to decide which unsuspecting guest would be signing on the dotted line as a client by the end of the night.

The groom's divorced, but friendly, parents sat in the front row weeping all over one another. If they didn't end up renewing their vows by the end of the month he'd eat his shoes. But they were already Damien's clients so they didn't count.

His own parents, the estimable Gilchrists, a couple who had taken the 'till death' part of their own wedding vows so seriously he wouldn't be surprised if they one day throttled one another, had naturally wangled the next best seat in the house: row two, on the aisle. They were no doubt the filthy-richest pair in the room, but they had never forgotten the year he'd lost all his pocket money running a secret Spring Racing betting ring while in middle school and thus wouldn't part with a cent of their precious dough. Talk about the ungettable get.

Damien's Aunt Gladys gave him a little finger wave from the fifth row. Caleb winked back and she all but fainted on the spot. He knew without a doubt she would have given him a perfume-scented cheque within five minutes of him courting her. But where was the thrill in that?

Masses of other faces he'd never seen and never particularly wanted to again soon passed him by in a Technicolor blur.

Until his brain slowly caught up with his eyes and he realised halfway down on the left side he'd passed over a swathe of long brunette waves, the immobilising combo of soft blue eyes fringed by impossibly long dark lashes, and the kind of soft, sweet, wide, pink mouth any sane man would kill for. Would die for.

Ava…

Her name launched itself smack bang in the centre of his unsuspecting consciousness from somewhere deep inside like a guided missile gone astray.

His eyes retraced their journey over the colourful crowd,

sweeping across row after row, even though he knew it couldn't have been her.

Well, logically it *could*. She *was* Damien's sister. But the groom had never once mentioned his sister was coming home from Boston for the wedding and for the first time in nearly a decade. If he had it was not the kind of crumb of information that would slip Caleb's mind.

But he saw nothing but a sea of unfamiliar faces, none of which made his stomach clench as hers did. Or more precisely as hers had. *Once upon a time in a galaxy far, far away…*

The last time he'd laid eyes on her he'd been a twenty-two-year-old business school graduate who'd been perfectly happy to bank on his family name to get where he was going. While she'd been a nineteen-year-old humanities wunderkind prepared to go to the far end of the earth to find a place where nobody knew her family name.

They'd been friends since high school, combatants just as long, and lovers for just one night, the day before she'd left to take up a scholarship at Harvard, the first of several top-class schools she'd flitted between since, and never looked back.

Never written a postcard, nor a letter, nor an email. No carrier pigeons had been employed by her, nor telephones rung on his behalf.

He frowned and curled his toes into his new black leather shoes until they hurt. He'd searched every pew and couldn't find the brunette waves, the smoky blue eyes, or the wide pink mouth. He must have imagined her after all. Great hulking fool he had always been when Ava Halliburton had been the subject of discussion…

'Caleb?'

Caleb looked at the groom blankly as a ripple of laughter washed over the crowd.

'You're on, buddy,' Damien said.

'On what exactly?'

'The ring?' Damien said, loaded smile playing about his mouth telling Caleb it wasn't the first time he'd been called.

'Right,' Caleb said. 'Apologies. I was a million miles away.'

And a million years ago.

'Not the kind of thing I want to hear right now.' Damien's smile didn't slip a millimetre but Caleb had known the guy long enough to know his patience was thinning.

Caleb slid a finger into a tiny side pocket of his waistcoat and pulled out a skinny white gold band encrusted with diamonds. He summarily dropped it into Damien's upturned palm lest it rub some of its unwelcome romance upon him.

From there the wedding zoomed to a brisk conclusion.

The kiss was the best part. Damien grabbed Chelsea around the waist, dipped her halfway to the floor and planted one on her that had the two-hundred-strong crowd whooping it up in the aisles.

That's my boy, Caleb thought, glad his friend wasn't becoming a complete sap now that he was locked down.

Caleb followed the couple down the aisle, arm in arm with Chelsea's sister, who he could see out of the corner of his eye was grinning at him. He feigned boredom as he stared blankly towards the bright light of a video camera at the end of the aisle.

'I was afraid you might be about to faint on us there for a moment,' Kensey said.

He let his mouth kick into half smile. 'Me? Faint? Simply not in me, honey.'

'So you're a fan of big white weddings, then?'

'Nowhere I'd rather be on a Saturday night.'

'Really? Must have been the way the light was hitting your cheeks that made you look like someone had walked over your grave.'

'Must have been,' Caleb said.

Though he couldn't help but look to the left in search of a pair of pretty sky-blue eyes and long dark hair.

Damn fool.

After a good long hour of photographs taken around the iconic Brighton beach huts, Caleb finally stepped out of his limo in front of the Halliburtons' house at the upper end of Stonnington Drive.

He stretched his arms overhead, let out an accompanying groan, and once the other groomsmen, Chelsea's brother-in-law and one of Damien's cousins, had moved on through into the house, he let his gaze swing straight to the second-floor window, third from the right.

Ava's bedroom window.

Between two beats of his heart he went from thirty-two-year-old man of enviable experience to twenty again, riddled with wild hormones and unable to help watching the sway of cream curtains flapping gently at the window, wondering if Ava was up there sleeping, studying, getting dressed, getting undressed…

Today the window was closed. No lights were on. His mind eased.

His hormones were another matter.

He jogged around the side of the massive house, hoping the exercise might relieve some of the tension he'd carried with him from the church.

The Halliburtons' manicured back lawn had been over-taken by two massive white brightly lit marquees. They draped languidly across the yard like decadent Bedouin tents. A ten-metre gap between them left a makeshift cork dance floor open beneath the stars. Fat pale purple bows were wrapped around the two-hundred-odd antique bronze chairs and the round tables were heavy with white roses, crystal glasses and gleaming silver cutlery.

He reminded himself not to stand directly below any of the dozen chandeliers. He was no engineer but he couldn't for the life of him figure out how the outrageous things wouldn't bring the whole deal crashing down upon their heads.

He took a deep breath, tucked his hands into his tuxedo trouser pockets and sauntered inside, familiarising himself with all exits, making instant friends with a passing waiter so he'd get first look in at the hors d'oeuvres, before making a beeline for the nearest bar.

He ordered something heavy and straight up. The burning liquid had barely touched his lips when an all too familiar female voice from behind him said, 'Caleb Gilchrist, as I live and breathe.'

His glass clinked against his teeth as he swallowed more than was entirely sensible on an empty stomach.

'Well, if it isn't little Ava Halliburton. In the flesh,' he said as he turned, a nonchalant smile already planted steadfastly upon his face.

And, oh, what a choice of flesh.

Her long dark hair hung from a centre part just as it had when she was nineteen, and it was still, oh, so sexily mussed, as though she'd spent hours running agitated fingers through it. Her blue eyes were luminous in a round face that had always made her look younger than she was. A naturally wide smile hovered cautiously upon her mouth and her cheeks were flushed.

The champagne glass between her fingers exposed fingernails bitten to the quick. She wore a shapeless, sleeveless dark pink lace dress that stopped square below her knees. It was offbeat, slightly too big and not quite formal enough for the occasion.

She hadn't changed a bit.

A distant relative of some sort appeared from nowhere to capture Ava's attention. She shot Caleb a quick 'I'm sorry' with her eyes before she turned towards much pinching of cheeks and 'I knew you when you were this big' remarks.

Caleb took a step away, towards the bar, where he put down his glass and gladly took the reprieve.

Ava Halliburton. It had been some time since that name had made him curl his fingernails into his palms.

At twenty-two, confused and smitten, and only hours after the most raw, tender, surprising night of his young life, he'd followed her to the airport, and five minutes before she was due to check in and fool that he was he'd asked her to stay for him.

And he'd been serious. In that crazy moment he'd been prepared to throw away the thought of ever being with another woman if he'd been able to have just her.

Because in her warm, willing arms he'd thought for the first time in his young life he'd truly glimpsed happiness.

Yep, happiness, that old chestnut.

And it had taken her about, ooh, half a second to refuse and take flight.

He braced himself to suffer the onrush of unbearable frustration he'd associated with her memory for a long time after she'd left him standing there in the middle of the airport terminal.

But the onslaught never came.

While she looked as if she'd stepped out of her high-school yearbook, the intervening years had changed him so much he was a different man. For one thing he was far less easily moved by things like loveliness and sweetness and sky-blue bedroom eyes.

If he were in the mood for romanticising things he might think *she'd* made him immune to all that, made him seek out the company of women who didn't have a chance in hell of touching him in that way. But he wasn't in such a mood. Therefore he decided that in the past ten years he'd been lucky to experience enough lovely, enough sweet, enough feminine eyes of every colour not to be so impacted as he had been by her, and by her leaving, ever again.

That was until Ava's spare hand, the one not swirling champagne hypnotically in its flute, reached up to finger a strip of thin brown leather at her neck.

A long thin strip of brown leather. One that looked a heck of a lot like one that once upon a time had accommodated a chunky wooden locket he'd given her as a birthday gift.

He'd put his photograph inside as a joke. She'd left it in there. For years.

The last time he'd seen the locket was on that night, the one night they'd spent together. Lying bundled up in a pile of clean towels and thermal blankets in a suspended shell of a canoe in the Melbourne University boat shed on a cold winter's night, basking in one another's afterglow, he'd opened it. Seen his picture. And his future. Or so he'd thought.

The idea that she might have yet to remove it dug in its claws and refused to be displaced.

Caleb's eyes remained riveted to the fingers playing with the leather strap. It lifted gently away from her creamy décolletage and then slid back against her. He wondered if the leather had been warmed by all that soft female skin.

The tips of his fingers began to tingle.

He followed the line of the necklace to find it dipped beneath the V of Ava's dress. There was no way of knowing what she kept there now, nestled between her breasts.

He allowed himself a moment to ponder the thought. Especially since in the past ten years little Ava Halliburton had filled out a little more than he'd initially realised. Even though he knew it a self-destructive thought he sent up a small prayer of thanks to the god who decided such things.

The cousin thrice removed moved on and Ava turned back to Caleb, remnant smile lingering upon her wide mouth. Suddenly her necklace didn't hold anywhere near as much fascination as those lips, which at some point in the conversation with Cousin Whoever had been moistened.

Caleb tipped back onto his heels. If he'd thought his fingertips were tingly they had nothing on his bottom lip. He dragged his upper teeth over it to stave off the sense memory lingering thereupon.

'It was a beautiful ceremony, don't you think?' Ava asked, turning side on, stealing away her leather strap, the V of her dress and her lips from his gaze as her eyes roved lazily over the noisily expanding crowd.

She was playing it beautifully cool, was she? Well, she'd just met the master of cool. *Ready yourself for a chill, kiddo…*

'Gorgeous,' he said, his tone glacial.

'And have you ever seen such stars?'

'When I have looked up. Sure.'

'It's such a perfect night for an outdoor reception.' Her nose screwed up. 'Though it will rain.'

'Do you have a barometer tucked somewhere beneath your dress?'

Her mouth twitched. 'Don't need one. The patch of cloud to the east. That's cumulonimbus cloud, the bringer of rain. But it won't come till late tonight. My parents wouldn't have had it any other way.' She leaned in ever so slightly and lowered her voice as she said, 'And did you get a load of the chandeliers?'

'You mean the insurance nightmare,' he shot back.

'Yes!' she said, turning to face him, grinning and pointing at his chest. 'That's just what I was thinking. They are a *Phantom of the Opera* intermission just waiting to happen.'

He laughed. True, it was only a soft cough kind of laugh, but it was a definite departure from cool.

Who was he trying to kid? He'd never been cool around this piece of work. What was the point? She could speak several different languages but the nuances of plain Australian cool went straight over her head.

Caleb straightened his shoulders until he felt a slightly uncomfortable warmth seep into his muscles, but it was enough to get him to start to relax. Relaxed was usually his permanent state. He never had to try this hard.

He turned his right knee toward her and leaned in. 'Let's hope for the wedding planner's sake it doesn't rain or your mother will no doubt refuse to pay while your father will hole himself up in his office for a month glad for the excuse to do so.'

Rather than getting a grin for his efforts, Ava's answering smile was toothless, and brief. The continuous swirling of champagne was also a good sign she wasn't feeling as bright and breezy as she was making out.

She was working as hard at this conversation as he was.

He looked away lest she figure him out as easily.

And where was the waiter with the hors d'oeuvres when he needed him?

CHAPTER TWO

'I'M REALLY glad I bumped into you tonight before things get too crazy,' Ava said.

'How crazy do you think they plan on getting?' Caleb asked.

'The DJ is a cousin of mine.'

'Right. So if he knows any music produced later than nineteen eighty-five we should be very much surprised.'

Ava smiled. Looked away. Looked back. 'Damien told me you were in New York late last year.'

That was some segue, he thought. 'That I was. It was a business trip. In and out.'

'I can't believe you never came out to visit. It's a forty-minute flight to Boston.'

'And a half-day spent at JFK. Time prohibitive.'

She nodded. Locked eyes. Swallowed. There was a husky note to her voice when she said, 'I missed you, you know.'

And just like that, with the faintest whisper of vulnerability, Ava turned Caleb's stoic resistance to putty. His tingling nerves burst into action, stinging the length of his fingers until he ached to reach out and touch her arm. To run his thumb over that full bottom lip. To hook a finger beneath that leather strap and slide its hidden secrets and regrets into the light.

Bad news. Little Ava Halliburton was nothing but bad news and it would pay to remember it. Just to hit the point home, through the pocket of his trousers he grabbed a pinch of leg hair and gave it a nice painful tug.

After her words had long since begun to fade into the noise around them, Ava cleared her throat and looked down at her shoes. 'I missed all of you guys. Heaps. Seeing everyone today really hit home how long I've been gone. My cousin the DJ was eight when I left and now...'

'Now he knows how to work a CD stacker like nobody's business.'

'Exactly.'

She glanced up at him from beneath those impossible eyelashes. He'd always thought them her best feature. But now they were running a pretty close tie with those wide smooth lips. He bit the inside of his cheek in penance.

Then said, 'It's nice to see you finally managed to peel yourself away from lectures and study groups for your brother's big day.'

A glint sparked within her sky-blue eyes and her lips widened, creating soft pink apples in her cheeks. Heaven help him.

'And just as nice to see you are no less of a buffoon than you always were. I can't believe Damo had to ask for the ring no less than three times. It will be *the* story they'll bring up every wedding anniversary for ever more.'

He gave a short bow. 'I aim to please.'

'Mmm,' she said, her eyes all too easily leaving his as she surveyed the room. 'I remember now you always were the kind of guy who liked to steal the limelight.'

She remembered *now*? How flattering. He said, 'While you always preferred to run from attention as though it might burn.'

The glint in her eyes flickered. Ever so slightly. But enough he knew he'd scored a hit. It felt less satisfying than he'd thought it would.

She brought her champagne glass to her lips and his obedient eyes followed. And then he saw that her left ring finger was clean and clear.

The last he'd heard she was meant to be living with a professor double her age or some such tale. It was one of many such tales he'd heard over the years, stories of inappropriate and much older men, of subsequent broken hearts and consequential school transfers from one side of the world to the other.

He wondered if running into Ava's 'plus one' was going to be his after-dinner surprise. He pictured some obscenely tall, grey-haired type with small glasses and a vocabulary built to keep ne'er-do-wells like him in their place.

At least by the look of things either the guy was a dud and hadn't given the poor girl the appropriate bling, or she was, in fact, as yet, still single.

He was a torn man deciding which was the more deserved outcome.

When he looked up she was watching him. More than just watching him—her eyes were roving slowly and carefully over every inch of his face.

When she noticed he had noticed, she smiled. 'I can see some things have changed. You never had stubble before.'

She reached out a hand but it stopped just millimetres short of touching him, the backs of her knuckles grazing nothing but air as she traced the contours of his face.

'It didn't occur to you to shave for the occasion,' she said.

Caleb took the opportunity to run his fingers over his stubble; the sting of short, sharp hair against skin was beautifully distracting to his other senses, which were on overload.

All that soft familiar hair, soft female skin, soft clouds of perfume he couldn't identify but knew he'd never forget;

those soft pink lips he'd kissed for the last time only moments before she'd walked away... Taking any naivety he might once have had with her.

'Nah,' he drawled, letting his hand drop to toy with his crystal-cut glass. 'I'm a rogue now, didn't you know? If I shaved I'd be unrecognisable.'

'Right. Wouldn't want to disappoint your public.'

The side of his mouth twitched into a smile despite itself. 'I've never been known to disappoint before.'

And where in the past she might have frowned, knowing there was a double entendre in there somewhere, and then blushed as she figured it out, this time her eyes slid back to lock with his.

She gave him a small smile to match his own. Then nodded, almost imperceptibly. Perhaps little Ava Halliburton had found time in her busy pencil-sharpening schedule to grow up after all.

'Be careful,' he said. 'You'll be on the business end of lots of pointing and staring and frowning if you stand next to me for too long. Your reputation will never be the same again.'

'I'll live.'

Caleb adjusted his stance as everything south of his thyroid felt fuel injected.

Before he had the chance to find out just how grown up she might yet be, she disregarded him in favour of looking up.

He tipped his head to see what was so great up there to find the stars were out in force, twinkling majestically through the gap between the two large swathes of white gauzy fabric that hung over the night.

Beside him Ava sighed. 'Did you know Galileo died in sixteen forty-two, the year of Isaac Newton's birth?'

Caleb grinned. Any other woman might have made a big

deal about the romance of the stars and the moon and the colour-tinted cake frosting… But not Ava. For all their history, and for all the niggling discomfort he felt not quite knowing where they stood with one another now, he couldn't deny she was one of a kind.

He leant his backside against the bar and crossed one ankle atop the other and asked, 'So how *is* school?'

After a few last lingering moments gazing at the dark sky, she dragged her eyes back to him. 'School's fine.'

'And what's your major? I can never keep up.'

'I'm nearing the end of my doctorate in Social Anthropology.'

'Meaning next time we see one another I'll have to call you Dr Halliburton? Marvellous.'

She didn't answer, just gave an indecipherable smile.

'And what does a doctorate in Social Anthropology entail exactly?'

'My paper is on consumption, gender and economic status among Manhattan adolescents.'

'Buying patterns of New York kids?' he asked.

Her smile was flat. 'It's not quite that simple. It's a study of ethnicity, family structure, peer pressure, needs versus desires, and identity.'

Spin it however she pleased, after her fancy-schmancy degree was finished little Ava Halliburton would be wanted by any American company that bought and sold goods and had a clue. Clever girl.

'So that answers my next question. You are still teacher's pet.'

Some unnamed emotion flashed across her eyes like quicksilver, but she lifted her chin and it was gone. 'If your memory stretches back far enough I'm sure you'll remember I was never the teacher's pet. I ask far too many obnoxious questions, which I've since discovered nobody really likes.'

Caleb laughed through his nose. And at the same time he felt muscles stretching that hadn't been used in years. Jousting muscles

For a guy who had things come all too easily to him all his life, Ava Halliburton had always been hard work. She'd never backed down from an argument. Never given an inch when she could take a mile. She was a challenge. And there was nothing Caleb liked sinking his teeth into more.

Down, boy.

'Have you seen your parents yet?' he asked.

She glanced down at her drink. 'I've so far managed to avoid that little reunion.'

He didn't half blame her. Since her parents' divorce she and her father had barely spoken, and her mother, though a delight to sit next to at a dinner party, was a Stonnington Drive cliché: ten per cent plastic, ninety per cent self-absorbed, and the last kind of creature who should ever have been allowed to be in charge of nurturing another living soul.

'And how are yours?' she asked. 'Merv and Marion still as surly as ever?'

'My mother has taken up pole-dancing.'

Ava's jaw dropped while her bright eyes danced. 'She has not!'

'That she has. Her doctor suggested it would be good for her blood pressure. As to my dad's blood pressure? I'd put money on the fact she gave that little to no thought whatsoever.'

Ava ducked her chin and smiled into her drink. When she looked back at him her head was cocked, that wide warm smile of hers was out in force, and Caleb felt the years just slip away.

'Are you staying here?' he asked, when the real question he wanted answered was would she be staying long.

'Hotel,' she said, shaking her head, thick dark hair cascading over her shoulders.

Caleb shoved his hands deep into his trouser pockets to stop from reaching out and brushing her hair back so that he could better see her face. She did always have such a charming face.

She glanced up towards the big house perched magnificently atop the great lawn. 'You know this is the first time I've set foot in this place in near on ten years.'

Nine years and four months. Caleb gritted his teeth until his jaw hurt, hating the fact that he knew that.

He'd lived more, bigger, harder, better in those nine years and four months than most men lived in a lifetime, yet the fact that Ava had not seen a day of it still left an indent somewhere deep beneath his ribs.

Out of the corner of his eye Caleb saw Damien waving frantically at him from the other side of the marquee. He was miming taking a photograph.

'Then I reckon you have a lot of catching up to do with a lot of people,' he said. 'I should stop monopolising your time.'

He squared his shoulders and took a step backwards, disentangling himself from the heady mix of cloying memories and Ava's faint but memorable scent. 'And it seems my best-man duties have barely begun. Are you sticking around?'

'Until the death,' she said, raising her glass to him.

'Fine. If I don't see you again before you go, it's been swell.'

'The swellest.' She smiled serenely, not giving away any kind of clue as to whether 'until the death' meant she was flying out at midnight or if she was back to stay.

Caleb shook his head to stop the ridiculous guessing games. It mattered to him not a lick either way.

He'd seen her. He'd talked. He'd been within touching

distance. And he'd survived. He'd more than survived. He'd remained blissfully untouched.

Well, as untouched as a man in the company of a beautiful woman could ever hope to be.

He leaned in to give her a kiss on the cheek. She lifted her face to him, a small smile lighting her features.

In the moment before his lips touched her cheek he felt as if he'd been smacked across the back of the head with a mallet as the close up image of long dark eyelashes fluttering against warm golden skin covered in the palest smattering of tiny freckles stamped itself upon his consciousness…

Waxing his boat late one evening. A sound. The scrape of a shoe on concrete. Turning. Ava, a shadow in the doorway. Tears glistening on those same cheeks.

And then the kiss. Their first kiss. Their first everything.

Her slim pale arms in the air, so trusting, as he slid her Greenpeace-emblazoned T-shirt over her head. The depth of feeling in her large eyes as she unclasped her bra. All that beautiful pale skin revealed just for him. Only for him.

Ava…

Once again her name shot through him, though this time it came to him like the first summer breeze: surreptitious, lingering, and a herald of delights yet to come.

He closed his eyes, rested his lips upon her cheek for the barest amount of time and did his best not to breathe through his nose. But the second it occurred to him he couldn't help himself.

With his first breath she smelled faintly of soap, of powdered make-up and of orange blossoms.

With his second he got schoolroom chalk, old library books,

and the fresh-cut grass at that spot by the Yarra where they'd gone every day one summer holiday to play backyard cricket.

And finally, most strongly, miles of freshly vacuumed carpet beneath his feet as he'd stood in Melbourne Airport's International Terminal, completely stunned to realise that she was really leaving him behind and leaving his broken heart trampled beneath her feet.

He pulled away and the delicious scent of powder and orange blossoms returned, leaving him wanting more.

And for a man who wanted for nothing, that was something. His was a life of wealth and success, of fast cars and fast women. Of the best of everything money could pay for. It was a life lived loud and hard, no apologies to anyone.

He should have thanked her. His drive, his detachment, his determination to win at all costs had sprung from the ashes of that long-ago day.

Ava Halliburton had made a man of him.

Yet as Caleb turned his back on her he hoped she had an airline ticket burning a hole in her purse.

Ava stood alone in the middle of the big white puffy wedding marquee, her heart pounding so loudly in her ears she was surprised she'd heard a word Caleb had said.

Coming home had been nerve-racking enough knowing she was set to confront those in her immediate family whom she hadn't spoken to in a long time. So she'd deliberately put Caleb to the back of her mind.

Caleb Gilchrist. The boy she'd hero-worshipped since she was fourteen. The boy who'd always pulled her plaits, had coined the nickname Avocado, which had stuck all through high school. Her brother's best friend. The devil on her shoulder. The thorn in her side.

Her first.

It was a good thirty seconds before she realised she was still watching him walk away.

She bit her lip and looked around her, sure that the strange guilty pleasure of it was written all over her face. But once she was sure nobody gave a hoot about the practical stranger in their midst, her eyes slid back to him.

The years had been good to him. Better than good. They'd given him shoulders a tailor would kill to dress. A mien of haughty condescension that oozed power and privilege. He wore his tuxedo with such authority and ease he could have given James Bond a run for his money.

He now had a jaw that she'd barely been able to keep from tracing. His ash-brown hair was cut short, hiding any evidence of its natural curl. And his dark hazel eyes, which had always been fuelled by a mischievous glint, were now lit by a very different fire. Confidence? Experience? Or a play-by-play photographic memory of their night together?

She closed her eyes tight on the reminiscence.

All that had been a long, long time ago. Eons. A lifetime. Yet a funny kind of energy skidded down her bare arms.

When she opened her eyes, she watched him chat with someone she didn't know. He smiled his killer smile and her chest tightened.

And she wasn't even a woman who was usually struck by so much obvious male beauty any more. She liked men who were…seasoned. Men whose suits bore elbow patches rather than designer labels. Men whose beards had grown in rather than men whose stubble made them appear downright wicked.

Her current man was of a generation that meant it had been some time since he'd had the kind of knockout rear view that made a girl happy to see him walk away.

Her man? Ha! For a moment she'd forgotten she was now

all alone in the world with no man to speak of. In fact, she wasn't sure she'd ever had a man in her life long enough to call him her man. Lucky for her she was smart enough to know why.

If her mother had been less interested in where she lived, how she dressed, and who knew about it, then she and her father would never have separated, their divorce would not have been as vicious and unexpected, and Ava would have gone out into the world feeling more safe, more secure, and less likely to run from every situation in which she felt herself getting sucked into any scenario even vaguely resembling a relationship.

Feeling like a wallflower, and one in need of a therapist if she didn't get her head sorted and fast, Ava began a slow weave through the space, hoping she at least looked as if she knew where she was going.

She smiled benignly at others she didn't know. People obviously important in her brother's life. It made her more than a little sad that she'd spent so much time away, and less than sure she'd made the right move in coming back.

To Stonnington Drive. A row of thirty homes, no more, but a stronghold all the same. It was the last bastion of the provincial old-fashioned good life to be found in what was now a relatively cosmopolitan city.

Stonnington Drive men wore suits long after they'd retired from high-powered jobs in the city. Stonnington Drive women believed in gin, tennis, and boarding school for the kids.

Ava believed it a suffocating, pulverising existence. The pressure to keep up with the Joneses, and the Gilchrists for that matter, had broken down her parents' marriage in the most vociferous, public, ravaging way. The run-on effect had left her searching for guidance wherever she could find it. And every day she'd been away from the place she'd thanked her lucky stars she'd managed to get out when she had.

For who knew at nineteen how strong one's principles really were? Another year there, another reason to stay, who knew…?

She glanced over to her brother to find Caleb had joined him. Damien had survived their childhood and made good. But he'd been older. Stronger. Luckier.

The two men put arms around one another as they ducked heads and talked. Best friends, even after all these years. As close as brothers. Closer even, considering her father had always treated Caleb like the second son he'd never had.

No wonder.

He was the perfect by-product of his upbringing: rich, good-looking, arrogant, lackadaisical. So she ought to have felt ambivalent in his company, despite their friendship all those years ago.

So why, now, couldn't she shake him off?

Because this place was insidious. It had a way of drawing people in with its luxury and its easy living and never letting them go. She felt her back teeth grinding and had to click her jaw open wide in order not to let it bother her.

Damien wrapped his arms around his bride and herded her towards the photographer, who was standing by a massive ice sculpture of a mobile phone. Ava felt a twinge of remorse that she had no idea what circumstances had led to what must have been some kind of crazy in joke in her brother's life.

Damien and Chelsea began to kiss, and didn't let up. It was so sweet. So romantic. Her stomach twisted. She had to look away.

A pair of hazel eyes snagged hers. Caleb again.

Guests' heads bobbed between them cutting off her view, but every few seconds that hot hazel gaze sliced through the air, unreadable at that distance, yet aimed directly at her.

She hadn't needed his earlier warning to take heed where he was concerned. It had taken no more than a second in his company to see that, just as she'd changed over the years, the boy she'd known, in all his varied incarnations, was no more.

There was apathy in his overly relaxed stance, arrogance in the angle of his chin, and the glimmer of barely restrained sensuality radiating from those disarming hazel eyes.

And despite the distance, despite the string quartet playing the perfectly respectable 'Clair de Lune', and despite the two-hundred-odd elegant party guests chatting up a storm between them, under his watch she began to feel warm and restless all at once.

She ought to have looked away. To have let her eyes slide past his as though she hadn't even noticed.

But after the month she'd had, having a man who looked like Caleb Gilchrist looking at her as if she were some kind of exotic dish he'd once tasted, and now was deciding if he wanted to go back for seconds, was like an elixir. Like a balm to the great gaping wound in her own self-worth she was trying her best to conquer.

She cocked her head in question. A leisurely smile lit his eyes. The heat of it leapt across the marquee and burned her cheeks.

She hadn't heard from him in nearly ten years. Yet she'd often wondered if he thought of that night fondly or with regret, or if he thought of it at all. Right then her question was answered; her old friend was not reminiscing about pulling her plaits.

Her heart responded, thumping hard and steady against her ribs, making her feel soft and breathless and interesting, not the great big loser with bad judgement in her past and big trouble in her future who'd jumped on the plane in Boston because spending time with her unhinged family had felt like the lesser of two evils compared with the situation awaiting her back at Harvard.

He made her feel as if her blood were so much lemonade. Always had. And it was the exact kind of feeling she needed right now.

She licked her suddenly dry lips and Caleb's smile grew until she could see a pair of pointy incisors. It was the slow, easy, sure smile of a predator who knew exactly what his prey was thinking. Ava was almost glad somebody did as right then she had no idea.

The hand holding the champagne glass shook ever so slightly. Enough so she sought out a table and placed the half-empty flute out of reach.

She turned away, ran her damp palms down the sides of her dress, spotted a gap in the crowd and went for it.

She hit the edge of the lavish white marquee and kept on walking, as fast as her low heels would carry her through the lush grass. She lifted her skirt, jogged up the steps at the rear of her parents' house and slipped inside.

And while everything outside had steadily made her feel as if she'd stepped into the Twilight Zone, inside the house was like déjà vu.

The walls were still panelled white below, pale striped wallpaper above, the floor still shiny blonde wood. Moonlight spilled in from discreetly angled skylights in the three-storey-high ceiling.

Memories swarmed over her, good and bad. But at least at last, for the first time since she'd left American soil the day before, she felt as if she was able to breathe again.

Coming home, even if only for a few days before she had to return to Harvard to front the Academic Review Committee, was the right decision.

Home was surely the only place to come to sort out her head, and her mess of a life, because this was where it had been all screwed up in the first place. It hadn't occurred to her that Caleb Gilchrist might play a starring role in the sorting. But if that's the way the fates wanted to play it, then who was she to argue?

CHAPTER THREE

CALEB glanced towards the big house. He'd last seen Ava heading that way. And any kind of conversation with her would be preferable to the one he was having right now.

Damien, Chelsea, Kensey and her husband Greg were talking about window treatments. Seriously, fifteen straight minutes of Caleb's life had been spent listening to the advantages of curtains versus wooden blinds.

Enough was enough. If he didn't get out of there and soon he might develop a tic. He'd already twitched every time the word 'shrinkage' had been uttered.

He clapped a hand on Damien's shoulder. And he bit down hard.

Damien ducked out of his grasp and turned with a frown. 'Whoa, buddy, you aiming to lame me just before my honeymoon?'

Caleb said, 'Did I mention I just ran into your sister?'

Damien had the good grace to look sheepish. 'You've seen Ava.'

'Unless you have another sister I didn't know about. Of course I've seen Ava! I know you have just had the biggest wedding this town has ever seen, but it was still pretty likely I'd notice your long-lost sister had made an appearance. It didn't occur to you to give me some kind of heads up?'

Damien slid Chelsea's champagne from her grasp, took a gulp, then his nose screwed up as the bubbles tickled his throat. He slid the glass back into her grip and she just kept on talking to her sister without noticing a thing. 'I don't know why I did that.'

'I do. You're avoiding the topic at hand.'

'Which was…?'

'The prodigal daughter has returned.'

'Right. Well, the truth is I wasn't sure if she was coming.'

Caleb left a big gaping hole of silent disbelief between them.

'It's true,' Damien said. 'She wasn't sure she could get away from school. She's smack bang in the middle of her doctorate, you know.'

'Yeah,' Caleb said. 'So I heard.'

'Well, then, what's the big deal? You had to assume she'd been invited.'

'Not good enough,' Caleb said, still finding it hard to simmer down. Especially after that long hot look he and the woman of the hour had shared across the crowded room. He hadn't imagined it. The electricity between them could have shorted out the dozen Swiss designed watches in between.

'Fine,' Damien said. 'The truth is, after what you told me I didn't want to get your hopes up. That afternoon at the bar just before I proposed to Chelsea—'

Caleb held up a hand to stop his friend from saying any more. He remembered full well what he'd admitted to Damien in a unseemly fit of empathy brought on by a mix of hay fever medication, a week of late nights covering for his love-struck business partner, and a rearing of the ugly head of some random lone romantic gene life hadn't yet managed to quash.

He hadn't thought it wise to tell his best friend that he and the guy's sister had done the horizontal tango in a canoe in the University of Melbourne boat shed the day before she'd fled the country. But he had admitted that he'd had feelings for her a long, long time ago.

In case Caleb was feeling particularly forgetful Damien added, 'If not for my screwball parents setting such a bad example of what a real relationship should be like you and I could be related.'

Caleb's hand moved close enough to Damien's mouth he had to lean back away from it. 'Thanks for the recap.'

Damien grinned. 'Any time. So how did the big reunion go? Did violins play, hearts dance, angels weep?'

'It was peachy. Not exactly as exciting as root canal, but more fun than test cricket.'

Damien's eyes narrowed. 'Like that, is it?'

Caleb smiled; no teeth, no humour.

'I go on my honeymoon in three days' time. Between now and then I'm going to need you around and I'm going to want her around. So promise me you'll play nice.'

Caleb took a stuffed mushroom from a passing waiter and said nothing.

'It's taken some kind of convincing to make my new bride believe not all families are as screwed up as hers. I don't need you two going at each other as you always did and spoiling the illusion for me, all right?'

Instead of dignifying Damien's comments with a response Caleb stared at a point in the middle of his forehead, turned up the volume of his voice and asked, 'Are you wearing make up?'

Damien's chin dropped and his eyebrows disappeared under his dark fringe. 'Are you kidding me?'

At her husband's raised voice Chelsea stopped talking and turned to join their little gathering. Kensey formed the last edge of the circle. And both women turned to look hard at Damien.

Caleb popped the mushroom in his mouth, grinned at his

friend and walked away. Out of the marquee and towards the house.

'Play nice!' Damien called out from behind him. 'For my sake, play nice.'

Caleb gave a small wave over his shoulder and made no promises.

Caleb rounded the corner of the Halliburtons' large foyer and found Ava sitting on the winding staircase, her legs drawn up to her chest, her arms wrapped around her knees, her ankles turned so that the toes of her silver Mary-Janes kissed.

Even though she had an empty stubby of beer dangling from one hand she couldn't have looked more like a little kid dressed up in her elder's finery if she'd tried.

When she saw him there she smiled.

'Hi,' she said, tilting the beer his way.

'Hi,' he said, pulling up short and tucking his hands into his trouser pockets.

Her smile, if anything, widened. And if she was any other woman, he would have thought by the coquettish look in her eyes the bottle in her hand swinging back and forth meant she was contemplating replacing one vice for another.

'We have to stop meeting like this,' she said.

'Ten years and not a word. Now twice in ten minutes. If I didn't know better, Ms Halliburton, I would think you were following me.'

'Hey, I was here first.'

'So you were.'

He smiled. She smiled some more. It was all far too civil-ised. It couldn't last.

'Any particular reason you've chosen to snub the fes-tivities?' he asked.

Her soft mouth slowly grew wider and wider until her face

was all about killer cheekbones and eye sparkles, and Caleb decided it best not to say anything remotely nice or amusing in the hopes she'd save that debilitating smile of hers for someone else.

'I'm hiding,' she said.

'From whom?'

'Family, basically.'

'Right. So have you caught up with your father yet?'

She bit her lip and looked straight through him for several seconds before blurting out, 'Aunt Gladys. I'm mainly hiding from Aunt Gladys. She's cornered me three times already with the aim of setting me up with her nephew Jonah. The fact that Jonah is also my cousin seems to have escaped her.'

'That's a tad alarming, even for Aunt Gladys.'

'I'll say. I figure if I stay out of sight she'll find some other poor sap to coerce.'

'Sounds like a plan.'

Caleb wondered why she hadn't just told Aunt Gladys she was with someone. The image of the lanky grey-bearded professor, who no doubt thanked his lucky stars daily for whichever man in her past had sent her into the arms of someone of his ilk, popped unwittingly into his mind. He mentally stuck out his foot and smiled inwardly as the figure tripped over his large shoes and fell face flat on the floor.

After that diverting little thought he figured now seemed as good a time as any to find out what the situation was.

'You didn't think to bring a date along to ward off randy family members?' he asked. 'Just in case I run into Aunt Gladys I'd love to be fully informed so that I can help you out any way I can.'

Ava blinked and her eyes suddenly seemed darker. 'I only arrived this morning. Not much time to rustle up a date. There was a guy washing windows at an intersection on the way from the airport. If only I'd been more on the ball.'

'If only.'

If only she would give him a straight answer.

Maybe what she needed was a straight question.

'So where's this professor of yours Damien told me so little about? Back at the hotel? Past his bedtime? Or did he not want to give up his nightly malted milk by the fire with his cat at his feet to come across the pond?'

'Yep,' she said, not looking at him. 'Something like that.'

She lifted herself off the step and wobbled a tad. Caleb wondered if that had been her first beer.

'So,' she said, head down, hair falling in a waterfall over her face as she scuffed her shoe against the step, 'which of the bevy of beautiful blondes out there under the stars is your arm candy for the evening?'

'Who says I have any interest in arm candy?'

She lifted her chin, her mouth twisted as she pinned him with her trademark flat, discerning, too-smart-for-her-own-good gaze. 'There is such a thing as email, you know. And from what I hear from those who've used said email to tell me things about home, these days you're a regular hound dog.'

Caleb laughed. The sudden explosive release of tension was such a surprise he let it rumble through him a good deal longer than he'd normally bother.

And it felt good. Really good.

It was enough to make him glad he'd sought her out again. For one thing she didn't seem to have an inordinate interest in Roman blinds. And for another he was definitely enjoying her attempt at being sassy. She honestly had no idea she looked as if butter wouldn't melt in her mouth.

'And what makes you think you can trust such stories?' he asked.

'The source.'

He glanced her way, eyebrow raised.

'My brother.'

Caleb laughed again. 'You can't be quoting your brother, I'm sure.' Damien would have used far less ambiguous language.

'I am,' she said. 'Or I think I am. He may have put things another way and I simply extrapolated that meaning. So you're not a hound dog?'

The minx actually looked disappointed.

'Honey, I'm not sure any man has been a "hound dog" since the nineteen fifties.'

'But—'

'But I understand your meaning. And he was quite wrong. I'm perfectly discriminating,' he said with a devilish smile.

'How's that? No blondes after Labour Day?'

'I said I was discriminating, not an imbecile.'

This time Ava laughed. Her eyes brightened, her hair shimmied, and those lips… Damn, but she was one gorgeous creature.

Caleb's extremities stirred as he wondered how long it might take for butter to melt anywhere else on her body.

'So anyway,' Ava said, before he could sink too deeply into that fantasy, 'I was thinking of heading up to my old bedroom for a nose around. See if my mother turned it into an aquarium, or a gift-wrapping room, or a yoga studio. What do you reckon?'

'Knowing your mother I'd say trophy room.'

Ava clicked her fingers. 'Right. Of course it is. So, do you want to come see if you're right?'

Caleb waited for the other shoe to drop, but she merely blinked at him, all ingenuous blue eyes.

Ava was inviting him up to her old bedroom.

It didn't mean what the sudden surge of adrenalin throughout his body indicated it meant. Or did it?

Only one way to find out for sure…

He placed his right foot on the bottom step and leaned in towards her, thus crowding her personal space to the point where he could see flecks of silver and navy in her irises.

And he waited for her to lean away. Or frown. Or run as she had run before.

But she didn't move an inch. She just blinked back at him until he could tell that an extensive array of wheels whirred madly in her head.

Every look, every move, every word that had come out of her mouth had been entirely deliberate. She knew exactly what she was doing. She'd done it all before…

Her arms in the air, so trusting, as he slid her Greenpeace-emblazoned T-shirt over her head. Her small hands tugging his T-shirt from his jeans. Her soft hands sliding around his waist…

Caleb's temperature began to soar.

Ava reached out and ran a hand over the carved sphere balanced on the end of the banister and said, 'You coming?'

He had never in his life wanted to be an inanimate lump of wood more. He waved a hand up the stairs. 'After you.'

Damien had asked him to play nice, after all.

Damien…

He shunted that particular name from his mind. This had nothing to do with his best friend and business partner. Nothing to do with the guy who'd taken him in and made him feel a part of a family the moment he'd realised Caleb's own family were as warm as a meat locker.

It never had. And it seemed it never would.

Ava gave a little curtsy, ducked her chin and smiled before jogging upstairs without looking back. It wasn't until she was halfway up that he came to his senses and followed.

She didn't even glance at the several other doors they passed, she just kept walking until they hit the third door from the end. It was closed. Her chest lifted and dropped before she grabbed the handle, turned and opened the door.

'Was I right?' Caleb asked.

She shot him a quick glance, and the smile that lit her face was as stunning as it was surprised. 'Not even close.' And in she went, leaving the door open for him to join her.

If he'd thought his body temperature was adversely affected by her before, now it was skyrocketing far too quickly out of his control for his liking.

One of the many things Caleb liked about himself was the fact that he was never out of control. Whether entertaining clients at a gentlemen's club, risking millions of dollars on one single stock market trade, or in the presence of a beautiful woman, he never let himself forget where he was and what *he* wanted from the situation.

All he could think to account for his current state was that he had not one single clue what he wanted from Ava Halliburton…

Her soft hands sliding around his waist. Her warm lips opening up beneath his. Her cool, naked body wrapped around him. The two of them joining. Sultry, hushed, tender joining. And all the pressure and hope and expectation that sat upon his shoulders each and every day stilled…

He shook his head to shatter the avalanche of memories overcrowding common sense.

You are two old friends, he told himself. *This has nothing to do with the last twenty-four hours you spent together; it has everything to do with the several years before that. Or the ten years since. You are both simply being pleasant. Re-*

forging ancient ties. For Damien's sake. Damien your business partner and best friend.

Ava poked her head back out the door and curled a saucy finger at him, then disappeared back into that which Caleb had once seen as the promised land.

If he truly believed they were simply being pleasant he was some kind of fool. And if he gave in to the invitation in Ava Halliburton's sultry blue eyes then he was an even greater fool. On a thousand different levels.

Nevertheless he turned the corner and followed her into the bedroom. Her bedroom. Kept neat and tidy and exactly as it had looked the day she left.

There Ava's bonhomie faltered. She glanced from him to the bed, which stood out like an albatross in the middle of the near wall. Then she shot to the other side of the room to open the bay windows, putting as much distance between them as she could.

Once the breath of cool night air took some of the edge off the heat simmering like a mirage between them, she relaxed again. And soon became engrossed in the hundred-odd books filling her childhood bookcase.

Caleb sauntered over to her dressing table, picked up a powder brush and sniffed. The scent was overwhelmingly familiar. Powdered make-up and orange blossoms.

It brought back a dozen memories. A hundred moments. It was sweet. Clean. And irresistible. It was her.

No other woman in the world smelt quite like that. Like innocence and loveliness and spring and whimsy. He'd been with enough of the female population to be quite sure. Not that he'd been keeping score.

He put the brush back where he found it and turned to find Ava picking out a book, opening the first page and beginning to read. He knew the rest of the world, including him, had slipped away the instant the first word on the page had sunk into her consciousness. She'd always been that way. Wholly engaged. Greedy for knowledge. Smartest in the room by a Melbourne mile.

He ambled away from the dressing table, sparing a longer glance at the frilly pink bed taking up the bulk of the room before his gaze shifted back to her, and he wondered how close he might be able to get before she remembered he was even in the room.

Her bedroom. Alone. With her. And that cruel, sweet, intoxicating scent.

She grabbed a hunk of hair, twisted it into a knot and held it atop her head and he wondered if he sank his nose into the skin below her right ear whether she might feel as soft and sexy as she looked.

The longer he spent watching her, the more he realised that he'd been kidding himself. The tousled, gangly dilettante of years past was no more.

Arcing smile lines book-ended the corners of her soft pink mouth and the frown lines above the bridge of her nose never completely went away. While the best curves now curved all the more, overall her figure had fined down as the last of her puppy fat had been eaten away by cold winters of the northern hemisphere.

And where the old Ava had curved self-consciously into herself, this Ava stood straight, shoulders back, hip cocked, sure of herself in a way Caleb wasn't certain he wanted to identify.

The Ava he'd known so briefly and lost so quickly all those years before had been exceedingly smart, but mostly a scared and stubborn girl.

This Ava was all woman.

Music from the marquee below filtered up through the night and wafted into the room. Shuffling cymbals, a moody piano, and a breathy male voice singing of foolish lovers.

She looked up from her book, blinked, stared for a moment through the bay windows, then smiled a sad smile. A smile heavy with experience. Innocence and whimsy suddenly didn't belong anywhere near the airless atmosphere of her bedroom.

Caleb realised his heart was thumping far too loudly in his chest for comfort.

'I love this song,' Ava said, her voice unnaturally husky.

She turned from the waist and looked his way, her smile soft and warm, her eyes hooded dreamily as she looked him in the eye with half her attention on the hazy melody echoing across the lawn.

Caleb didn't look away. He couldn't. Hell, he didn't want to. He simply let himself drink in the sight of her. Those piercing blue eyes. That fringe of sooty lashes. The heavy dark hair cascading over her shoulders.

Until that moment, Caleb didn't even know there was such a thing as perfect shoulders. Hers were lean, shapely, pale as porcelain with curves and crevices in all the best places.

She sucked her wide lips between her teeth, looked down at her hands, only then remembered the book she was holding, and furrowed her brow ever so slightly. She shut the book with a loud snap, then reached around to slide it back into place on the bookshelf, angling her head so that Caleb realised that her neck was pretty damned near perfect too.

He was so mesmerised by all that beautiful pale skin glowing in the moonlight spilling through the bay windows, along with the obscenely romantic music, that he didn't realise she was walking towards him until the scent of orange blossoms made his nostrils flare like a stallion in heat.

'Don't you love this song?' she asked.

Song? There was a song playing?

There must have been. She was swinging her hips, her chin was tilted down so that she was looking up at him from beneath her lashes, a small smile playing about her mouth. The music slowly wound its way back into his consciousness.

She held her hands towards him, palms up. 'Dance with me. For old times' sake.'

He'd been around the traps long enough to know that a dance wasn't all she was after. One of them had to be level-headed. What a great pity it had to be him.

'Ava,' he began.

But she held a finger to her lips and swayed up to him, taking one stiff hand and placing it in hers, then taking the other and winding it around her waist until it rested on her back.

If he moved his little finger an inch it would meet the curve of her buttocks.

Caleb closed his eyes and prayed for forgiveness.

That was the last time in some time that he thought of anyone else bar the woman in his arms.

CHAPTER FOUR

THE slow beat of the music was seductive. But Caleb still fought against giving in to the undermining scent and softness assailing him.

As was her nature Ava led. Or at least she tried to.

As was his nature Caleb couldn't let her. Mentally cursing himself as he did it, he slid his arm far enough around her that she was pressed bodily against him.

After he'd spent an excruciating minute trying his best to keep his steadily building desire from spilling over into anything slipperier than just dancing, Ava tipped her head back and looked into his eyes.

'Hi,' she said.

'Hello again,' he returned.

'This is nice.'

Nice? She thought the vertical foreplay they were so casually indulging in was *nice*? He thought it was pretty much akin to madness!

'We could do this downstairs, you know,' he suggested. 'Where there is an actual dance floor just for this precise purpose. Under the stars you were so taken with earlier.'

Ava screwed up her nose. 'I hate dancing in public. I have two left feet.'

True, Caleb hadn't been taking all that much notice of her feet until that point, what with all of her other parts vying for his attention.

His voice was a good note lower when he said, 'You're not doing a bad job of it right now.'

Ava snuggled closer until all of her soft bits curved all too neatly against his hard bits, and he had to grit his teeth to stop throwing her over his shoulder and carrying her to the bed and ravaging her senseless.

'Neither are you,' she said brightly, oblivious to the volcano building inside him. 'Have you had lessons?'

'Dance lessons?' Caleb cringed. There he was feeling like Valentino and she saw Fred Astaire. 'Ah, no. I was born with unparalleled natural grace.'

'Were you, now?' Her smile was sultry as all get out and Caleb was almost undone.

'Just shut up and dance, will you?'

'Yes, sir.'

He pulled her closer so that her head rested against his chest. Her hair slithered against the bottom of his chin, but at least he didn't have to look down into those smoky eyes, or be within kissing distance of those heaven-sent lips.

The song came to an end. The echoing cheer of a happy crowd seeped into the room from the party below and finally they stopped swaying.

The honourable thing to do would be to extricate himself from Ava's arms, to bow out of whatever game she was playing and leave her room, get back to his best-man duties and keep his hands and every other part of his anatomy well enough away from the groom's sister.

But Caleb didn't do any of that.

If anyone at that wedding had the notion that he might be an honourable man, they had another think coming. True, he didn't lie, cheat or steal, but he did push the boundaries of respectability on a daily basis.

If he knew a client had a penchant for wet T-shirt contests he would and had found the best Melbourne had to offer if that was what it took to get them to choose him over any other firm. He'd dated women, and the next week dated their room-mate. He risked millions of dollars of other people's money every day and did so without flinching.

Because he had a burning desire to win. To get what he wanted. To never again hear the word no and let it break him down to his very essence. Even though he knew he could build himself up again. He'd done it before. It just hadn't been all that much fun.

As to what he wanted in that precise moment? There was one thing he was not going to deny himself...

He pulled away. Ava's head lolled back and when she looked up at him her eyes were drowsy and dark, her lids heavy, her everything as sexy as hell.

'I've been itching to do this all night,' he said.

Her eyes widened, her view focused and she swallowed. Hard.

Caleb let go of her hand. Hers fluttered to rest against his shoulder with the delicacy of butterfly wings.

His free hand stole around her neck, his thumb running slowly along her clavicle.

Her breath caught. Her breasts pressed against his chest. Her pupils grew so large there was barely a speck of blue left within.

He gently slid his fingers beneath the leather strap, slowly lifting it off her neck and from beneath her dress until the pendant it held peeked over the top.

The locket.

The locket he'd bought her for her sixteenth birthday.

She was still wearing it.

Caleb didn't know whether he ought to feel uncomfortable or wholeheartedly smug.

He stared at the clasp, visualising opening it to see if the picture of him winking at the camera still held pride of place within. But going that next step would have given too much away. More even than he wanted to admit to himself.

He was rather glad that he had suddenly found other more pressing things to concentrate on.

Like how warm the skin of her neck felt beneath his knuckles.

Like the fact that her breaths were coming harder and faster, pressing her torso closer and closer to his.

Like the small crease at the edge of her lips that was just begging to be kissed.

He let the pendant go until it swung between them; cool, closed and jammed full of memories. Memories that did not span any of the past ten years. Because she had left. Without looking back.

She's all grown up, he reminded himself. *She's no longer the innocent who came to you looking for deliverance all those years ago.*

But just as he knew he was made of stern enough stuff to rise again after any setback, he also knew it was in her nature to run when the going got tough. It would pay to remember that. He had few serious qualms about seeing where she was going with this little seduction scene of hers but emotional detachment was paramount.

Then he looked into her eyes.

She was smiling. The little vamp knew exactly what he was thinking.

He raised an eyebrow in question. She did the same just as her hand slid around the back of his neck, kneading the tops of his shoulders until he felt like purring.

Another song started up. This time the slow, easy, lazy

strum of an electric guitar. Echoing, rumbling, bass deep notes vibrating through his bones.

The thumb of her other hand stroked the inside of his palm with such dexterity he felt it in the backs of his knees.

And just when Caleb thought things couldn't get any better Ava pulled him close and she kissed him. Open mouth. Exploring tongue. Eyes closed tight. Body pressed hard against his.

Ava...

It took about a second and a half of half-hearted resistance before he joined in boots and all.

She tasted like lemon meringue pie and spring sunshine. Her hair beneath his hands felt like silk tumbling through his fingers. And the faint mewling sounds she made as he kissed her were to the tempo of his heart like a shot of epinephrine.

The kiss lasted thirty seconds at most, yet he'd never felt more turned on his whole life. She felt like a woman, she kissed like a woman, and it only made him hunger for her like a man.

When she pulled away her eyes were dark, unreadable. However, she was smiling and that was enough for him. He bent to kiss her again but she turned her head.

It seemed Ava had ideas of her own. She slid a finger into his bow tie and gave it a little tug. The back of his neck stiffened instinctively in response and her smile only widened. Whatever game it was that they were playing was getting more complicated. The rules were smudging as the furtive fun overtook rationality.

He couldn't walk away now. Especially when it was either this or choosing which he preferred: sphere-ended curtain rods or fleur-de-lis.

Sure, as if that made a lick of difference. If a chorus line of half-naked dancing girls appeared out the window at that moment he wouldn't have cared.

Ava tucked her tongue between her teeth as she concentrated on sliding his bow tie undone. It fell apart in her hands. He didn't blame it. The buttons of his shirt were next. Pop. Pop. Pop.

And then her hands delved into the gap in his shirt to perform long, languorous strokes across the skin of his chest. Sliding around his waist. Scraping down his back.

Academically Caleb liked the idea of a woman seducing him rather than the other way around as much as the next guy would. But being there with Ava had nothing to do with academics. Not for him anyway.

This was a dangerous game she'd started and he had every intention of showing her just how dangerous he could be. He was far too jaded now for her to ever affect him the way she once had, but he had every intention of blowing her mind.

And for that to happen it was time for him to take charge.

He spun her on the spot until her back was tucked in against him. She lost balance. He steadied her. Listened as her sharp breaths split the silence, a soundtrack to the burgeoning desire running thick and fast between them.

He waited until she softened and leaned into him. Pliant. Willing. His to guide.

Her ready supplication to his will brought back a flurry of memories of their first time. Sweet, soulful, gentle memories.

He shut them down.

If she wanted sweet and soulful tonight she'd come to the wrong place. She'd worn the wrong dress. She'd kissed the wrong man.

He slowly, slowly brushed aside the swathe of hair from her neck and pushed the strap of her dress aside, revelling in the faint tremors distinguishing her next breaths as he exhaled against her skin.

Then he sank his teeth into the tendon joining her perfect shoulder with her perfect neck. The most insanely delicious taste exploded on his tongue. Like fresh milk and hot skin and potential.

He bit down again, this time closing his eyes to all other sensations as he tasted her with his tongue. Oh, God, she was as smooth as honey and cream and milk chocolate and all things bad and decadent.

Had she tasted this good the first time? If so, how could he possibly have forgotten?

With every slow nip and lick of her shoulder she sank further against him as though her knees were about to give way.

Her hands quivered against his thighs before taking purchase. Clinging to him. Making his every muscle contract and ache for more.

An inch closer to his zipper and she would have felt exactly how turned on he was.

He bit her earlobe and she groaned. He wrapped his hand in her hair and tugged her head back to get better access and her mouth fell open with desire.

Her reactions were all instinct and honesty. Nothing held back. It was intoxicating. She was enchanting. He was fast forgetting how cynical he was about such things.

And they'd barely begun.

He had no doubt a lesser man than he would have been apprehensive about living up to the intensity of the heat between them. Lucky for him, and even luckier for her, he was not a lesser man.

He traced the edge of her dress with a searching hand. He found her zip and slowly, agonisingly slowly, slid it open. The sound grated against his nerves like fingernails down a blackboard.

The fabric flapped aside revealing even more pale, perfect skin and shoulder blades right up there with her shoulders and neck.

It was then he realised she wasn't wearing a bra. A sound something along the lines of 'Phwoar' escaped his lips before instinct kicked back in.

The backs of his knuckles caressed her naked back. The bumps of her spine. The scar where she'd cut herself on an overhanging tree branch when hiding out by the fifth tee of the nearby golf course as a kid.

The past and the present slammed together so fast he could barely remember what the word detachment meant.

As though she'd sensed his hesitation, Ava turned her head, pressed a hand against his cheek and drew his lips back to hers. The kiss was sweet, gentle, slow, almost innocent and at the same time erotic as all get out.

Oh, to hell with it, he thought. *What the lady wants…*

She twisted in his arms, and he shucked the dress from her shoulders. A trail of goose bumps following in the wake of his touch.

Her responsiveness was astounding. She made him feel as if every touch was a caress. Every look a proclamation of desire. But he remained in control. He always did.

She stepped away, her dark eyes locked to his as her dress snagged on her hips. And all semblance of control flew out the window.

The Ava he once knew tangled with the changes that nearly ten years had made. Her lean, mean, girlish figure now curved delicately in and out in all the right places.

Caleb felt himself turning blind with lust.

As he drank in the sight of her she tossed her hair. But not with arrogance. Her fists clenched and unclenched at her sides. Her trembling was no longer purely a measure of simple pleasure.

Again her vulnerability snagged him. For a moment he tried to second-guess why she wanted this.

But then he remembered why he wanted it. She was woman. He was man. Period.

He looked back into her eyes, made sure she was hooked, then he gave her the full-glint treatment. 'Tell me I'm not dreaming.'

She slowly shook her head, a small smile tickling at the corner of her luscious mouth. 'You're not dreaming.'

'Then what the hell am I waiting for?'

He took two steps towards her, slid a hand into her hair and kissed her. Her breasts pressed against his naked chest. She slid her hands into his short hair and closed her eyes.

His vision blurred until all he could think about was skin and pink and visions of what else lay beneath what suddenly seemed like way too much dress for comfort. Her softness and sweetness was almost unbearable. Almost.

He kept his head as he backed her up against the bed. Her knees hit the mattress. She fell backwards. He landed beside her.

He was still lucid when he kissed his way down her body, taking his time to get to know every glorious turn of her breasts before moving down to her belly.

When her hands gripped the pink floral bedspread as he took the edge of her dress between his teeth and began pulling it past her hips his self-control remained in check. But only just.

The edge of her pants peeked back at him. White. Lace. Tempting. Taunting. His nostrils flared, blowing hot air across her lower belly, and she jerked towards him.

And for the first time in his life he found himself trying to keep up with the pure sexuality of a woman rather than the other way around.

When he touched her it was as though he were being touched. When he kissed her belly he felt liquid fire in his own belly. The scorching heat that surged through him as he slid a hand beneath her skirt and caressed her velvet-soft skin was irrational.

He was still fully clothed, for Pete's sake. Yet he was aroused to the point of agony.

The scrap of lace keeping her from his touch was laughable. He teased the edge with a feather-light caress and her eyes closed tight.

But he wanted her to know exactly who was putting her through this. 'Ava, open your eyes.'

They fluttered open. Took their time focusing. His pulse throbbed through his body as he waited for the catch in her breath, the surrender in her eyes, the acknowledgement in her smile that she was ready for the night of her life.

But they never came.

Instead she said, 'The average bed is home to over six billion dust mites.'

'No worries,' he said with a diabolical grin. 'You can be on top.'

Her throat worked. Several small frown lines appeared above her nose and then her hands pressed gently against his chest, the international sign for 'stop'.

Something had shifted within her. She was no longer the willing participant, and even less the instigator she had been mere moments earlier. Heck, she was so susceptible two more minutes and he would have had her spiralling into oblivion.

Two more minutes. Never before had so little time seemed so close. Yet so far away.

He slid his hand back into the light, pressed himself away from her, knowing the only way to think straight was to get his hands off all that gorgeous warm skin.

When he looked into her eyes instead of wildly passionate she suddenly looked panicked.

She might as well have doused him in a bucket of iced water for how quickly the haze of lust shrouding his judgement dissipated.

He moved so that no part of her touched any part of him. And she couldn't have hurried to disentangle herself from him faster.

By the time she sat upright on the edge of the bed her dress was held to her chest, her hair a mess, her knees clenched.

He ran a fast hand through his hair, reached out to her, then pulled his hand back to his side.

He was a selfish beast at the best of times, thus not any good at making other people feel better. Unless she could be assuaged with a flip remark, indulgence in more of what they had been doing, the inside news on a good trade, or a member's key to any of the top private clubs in town, he wasn't the guy for this.

'Ava, honey,' he said, his voice hoarse and stilted, 'are you okay?'

Her distant eyes lingered on his open shirt before she held up a hand, and said, 'I just need a minute.'

A minute? Boy, was she cool when she needed to be.

He buttoned the bottom two buttons of his shirt with thick fingers as he shot to his feet and paced to the far side of the room and back again and tried to figure out how he'd ended up there. With Ava. Rebuffed. Again.

His voice was cool as a suburban pool in winter when he asked, 'What was that all about, then?'

She shook her pretty head. 'Nothing.'

He pointed at the half-open bedroom door. 'Sweetheart, you bringing me up here and jumping my bones while there are two-hundred-odd people including your family just outside and after not seeing me for ten years is not nothing.'

She looked up at him. Glared, more like. But that was fine. It was much better to be on the end of that kind of expression than the self-loathing he'd seen in her eyes earlier.

'I didn't!' she said. 'I just needed... You wouldn't understand.'

'Try me.'

She bit her lips.

He ran a hand across the back of his neck, which felt hot and itchy. That was the feel of his self-protect mechanism finally whirring back to life.

'Ava, speak now or for ever hold your peace.'

'I… Just thanks, okay? It was just what I needed.'

Well. He'd wanted a straight answer, hadn't he?

CHAPTER FIVE

'JUST what you needed?' Caleb repeated, sounding as dumb-founded as he felt. 'Is foreplay the latest craze in jet-lag cures?'

'Maybe it should be,' she shot back.

'Ava,' he warned.

Her brows flattened, her mouth twisted. Then she shook her shoulders like an actor in the wings after a particularly difficult stage performance. 'It's just,' she began, 'the past month has been just so humiliating I can't even… Taylor and I broke up. So I left. And now I'm here. And I barely knew a soul out there under the marquee, which was only more depressing, as it only made me wonder why I came back. But then there you were…'

Her voice petered out. And no wonder.

She'd been using him. From the get go.

'Taylor?' he managed.

'My boyfriend. Ex-boyfriend.'

'The professor.'

Her mouth dropped open and she made true eye contact with him for the first time in an age. 'How did you—?'

'I am in contact with your family even if you're not.'

'Right. Of course you are.' When she looked back at him her eyes were luminous. 'We're cool, right?'

Cool? *Cool?*

'Sure,' he said cool dripping from his every word. 'Why be a best man unless you're guaranteed a tumble with the desperate, beer-soaked sister of the groom on the rebound?'

She threw her hands in the air with such gusto his tirade stopped at his throat. That same throat swelled shut when he saw actual tears glimmering in her eyes.

'I'm sorry, all right?' she said. 'Are you happy now?'

'Deliriously. You?'

'Oh, yeah. Beyond belief. My life is so-o-o peachy keen. You want to know why he dumped me? My so-called partner was offered a position on the Academic Review Committee, the committee charged with monitoring the progress of students attempting higher degrees. And with my doctorate in the pipeline he saw our situation as an ethical clash.'

Her bottom lip began to quiver and Caleb dug his toes into his shoes to stop himself from moving a muscle in her general direction.

And then she said, 'He chose the school over me.'

The parallel was priceless. Surely there was some kind of cosmic balance at play after the way she'd left him standing in the airport, but though the opportunity was ripe, and though he was feeling pretty darned indignant, he couldn't make himself say it.

When did he become so soft? When Ava Halliburton butted her pretty face back in his life, that was when.

'Damo's wedding must have felt like auspicious timing, then. What better a chance than to come home to lick your wounds?' he offered, hoping she might deny it, might still have some other reason up her sleeve for the sudden sexpot act. Like that he was simply irresistible.

But she looked up at him with a small smile on her face and nodded, as if the fact that he figured her out so easily was a good thing.

Well, damn her. Damn her and her perfect shoulders and her soft lips and the spell that she could still cast over him even though he knew damn well better than to fall for it.

He scratched the sudden itch at the back of his neck. Being around her, the move was becoming quite a habit.

'And then when you saw me coming you must have thought all your luck had come at once. You thought, Old Caleb's good for a quick roll. He's been there and done that and sold the rights to the T-shirt. He'd be the perfect means to getting my groove back.'

'No!'

'No?' he said, his voice dropping, no longer able to control his infuriation. 'You didn't think I'd be good for a quick roll? A slow roll, perhaps. A take-our-time-and-savour-every-second-as-we-take-all-night roll. Rolls so many and varied you'd wake up tomorrow unable to remember Professor Egghead's name. If you'd given me enough time I promise I could have surpassed your expectations back there.'

He waved an arm in the direction of the bed, which was messed up just enough anyone looking in would be in no doubt of what had happened. A spark relit the warmth in his veins and he realised how much he wanted her still.

Ava swallowed hard and looked up at him with those big blue eyes. Eyes that all too recently had been feverish with desire were now careful. She sniffed. And just looked at him. As if she were seeing him for the first time.

And though her hands were now wringing, and though her bottom lashes were still spiky with unshed tears, there was knowledge in her gaze. Pure, stark, feminine insight.

She saw right through him.

Her gaze dropped to the open neck of his shirt. She took one slow, shallow breath, then licked her lips. As though she wasn't nearly done with toying with him for her own emotional needs.

He was pretty sure she had no idea the power of the signals she was giving off. They were too pure. Too artless. And she was obviously feeling too mixed up and raw.

He knew then that if he took three long strides to her side and gathered her in his arms there would be no more waiting. The girl, the *woman* he'd wanted again for as long as he could remember would willingly be his all night long.

But a girl like Ava always came with strings. Far too many strings.

A burst of screeching laughter split the loaded silence, followed by stomping footsteps, and it was obvious that another pair of party guests had the same idea they'd had and were looking for an empty room in which to finish the thought.

That was enough to pull Caleb from his daze. He smartened up. Found his nerve. Packaged the whole evening into a tight ball and filed it deep down inside himself in the folder marked 'bad experiences best buried'.

'Come on, Doc,' he said. 'Let's get back to the party. I have a pretty speech to make before the night is out and no doubt Aunt Gladys has sent out a search party for you by now.'

Ava nodded. Straightened her back. Squared her shoulders. Stood. Smoothed her dress.

She looked his way. A flicker of guilt now etched across her beautiful face. Thank. Oh, no.

Caleb was no longer going to allow himself to be moved by her. Not in any way, shape or form.

If that day at the airport nine years and four months earlier had set him on the life's path of living big, living well and living alone, then this disaster of an evening had sealed it.

Big, bad, shrewd, imperturbable Caleb Gilchrist was back. Kicking butt and taking names.

* * *

Ava zipped her dress, ran a finger around the edges of her lips to fix her lipstick, tidied her hair and tried to ignore the sounds behind her.

But it was no use. Each noise only served as a reminder of the fact that she'd just tried to re-enact a night a long time ago when making love with Caleb had made everything in her life crystal clear.

Yet this time when she'd come to him looking for clarity, or even a little comfort, she had failed dismally.

And no wonder. The funny, sharp boy she'd always had a little crush on had become some kind of beautiful, which had caused her fuzzy synapses to snap.

The slide of buttons slipping through the button holes of Caleb's snowy white shirt reminded her of how strong and solid he'd felt beneath her hands. The rustle of tucking his shirt back into the beltline of his tuxedo trousers reminded her how liberating it had felt to tug them out in the first place.

She swallowed hard. Closed her eyes. And tried to think about something else…

Sliding open the door of the university boat shed, looking for her brother to tell him that the next day she might well be leaving to take up the full scholarship to Harvard she'd been offered.

Finding Caleb instead, alone in the half-darkness, waxing the hull of his row boat. Long-sleeved T-shirt rolled up to his elbows and clinging to muscles she hadn't ever realised he had.

Eyes dark as he'd turned and seen her there. Eyes narrowed as he'd realised she was upset. And the flash of awareness she'd felt as he'd taken her in his arms to comfort her.

Raining kisses over her face, taking away her tears. Feeling such certainty, such trust as he'd lifted her arms above her head and rid her of her T-shirt.

*The power surging through her as she'd unclasped her bra
and felt his eyes on her. The revelation. The power.*

*Touching, caressing, all that warm, damp skin and those
hard, lean limbs. The moment of pain when they'd first come
together. But he'd been so careful, so gentle, yet so sure, the
pain had soon been lost in the waves of pleasure so extraordinary she had been completely swept away...*

Ava's body still thrummed every place he'd touched.
Everywhere he'd kissed. Every other spot his warm breath
had caressed.

She opened her eyes and stared at a blank spot on the wall.
Was that what she'd been seeking from him again? The kind
of pleasure that would make her forget her life for a brief
while? If so, was that really such a lot to ask of a guy like
Caleb Hound Dog Gilchrist?

She shook her head, shutting out the sense memories. She
was a 'boyfriend' girl, not 'affair' girl or 'one-night stand' girl.
The length of time it had taken her to get over Caleb after the
first time proved that.

The first time together there had been a moment as she'd
lain in his arms when he'd played with her locket, smiled at
his picture still therein. In that moment if he'd asked her to
stay, rather than as an afterthought at the airport the next day,
her whole life to this point would have been different. Harvard
would have been forgotten. She would never have travelled
and studied at several of the world's top universities. She
never would have experienced different cultures and different men and been able to create a realm of knowledge from
which to gain perspective on life.

At best they might have stayed together, married and
bought a house near their parents. And she would have
become one of *them*. The dreaded Stonnington Drive wives.

At worst she would have had to watch the boy she worshipped move on to someone cooler, prettier, easier to love.

Either way she would have been the unhappiest woman on the planet.

But he'd dropped the locket back to her chest and thus let her go. He'd given her release. And the courage to spread her wings.

Caleb Gilchrist had been a pain in her behind her whole adolescence. He'd been her first crush just as long. He'd been her greatest awakening, sexual and otherwise.

And now? Now he was all shoulders, and a perfectly etched jaw line and a rear view for the ages. He wasn't as easygoing about the whole 'friends with benefits' thing as his reputation had made her hope he'd be. And the resultant embarrassment was quite simply the cherry on the top of what had been the worst month of her life.

'Ava,' Caleb said, his thick dark voice carrying to her across the room.

She turned to find him looking immaculate. Sleek. Unruffled, as if he'd been in this exact situation a hundred times before.

When she'd imagined him over the years he usually came dressed in jeans, a T-shirt, likely with a tear in the collar, and a baseball cap to hide his adorable ash-brown curls—the epitome of trust-fund-baby cool. That Caleb she'd been able to mock, to joke with, to like.

This Caleb was beyond her experience, varied as it had been. He was too strong, too cool, too sure of himself. She was pretty sure any teasing would bounce off him like a penny off a well-made bed.

Why hadn't she realised all that before she'd enticed him up here with half-baked hopes he'd be happy enough to do whatever it took to make her feel halfway desirable again?

His brow furrowed for a moment, and his mouth jerked at the corners,

So, so beautiful…

She ducked her chin. The fact that he'd even kissed her back meant she'd got what she'd come for. Enough was enough.

'So,' he said.

'So,' she said.

'They'll be serving dessert soon enough. Bacio Bacio's cinnamon gelato is the second reason I agreed to do this gig.'

Ava's mouth twisted into a half-smile that surprised even her. 'Plain vanilla is the world's favourite flavour of ice cream, making up twenty-nine per cent of all sales,' she found herself blabbing.

'Thank goodness you went to all those fancy schools.'

'I read that on the back of a packet of ice-cream cones.'

Laughter lit his eyes even if he didn't let it out. 'Shall we?' he asked, holding out his hand.

She had no idea what she'd done to be lucky enough not to be treated as if she were some misguided harpy. She opened her mouth to tell him so, then decided it would be best not to push her luck.

She put her hand in his. Such a large hand. It enveloped hers in warmth. And made her feel as if she wasn't as alone as she had felt an hour earlier.

If only she had realised that was all she'd needed before she'd invited him up here. Hmm. Deep down inside, in places she wasn't likely to tell another living soul about, she was actually rather glad she hadn't.

He tugged her towards the door.

'Wait,' she said, tugging back.

His altered expression told her his cool was waning.

'I am really sorry,' Ava said.

'Yeah,' Caleb said. 'So am I.'

They headed out the door and down the stairs in silence.

A tall silver-haired man walked past the bottom of the staircase. Ava's Mary-Janes squeaked on the carpeted stairs.

'Stop. Wait,' she whispered. 'It's my father.'

Caleb didn't even falter. 'Then you'd better get your game face on.'

Oh, no…

'Ralph,' Caleb called out as he dragged her onwards. 'How's it hanging?'

Ava saw her father's face light up before he'd even looked up the stairs.

'It's hanging just fine, son.'

He turned with an easy smile, winking at Caleb. Winking. Ava was pretty sure she hadn't seen her father wink since she was a little kid.

And then he saw her. If the refrigerator lost power, the sudden chill in Ralph Halliburton's face would still have kept the vodka happy.

'Ava,' he said. His voice gruff.

'Hi, Dad.'

He glanced between the two of them, then up the stairs, then back again. Her stomach sank so fast she felt it land somewhere in the vicinity of her ankles. And she felt a sudden need to check that her dress wasn't hooked into her undies.

When her father said not another word, Caleb leapt in. 'Having a good time tonight, Ralph?'

'Lovely time, thanks, Caleb. And you?'

'The mini quiches were an anticlimax, but apart from that the evening has been illuminating.'

Ava felt a tingle of alarm trickle down her spine. She crushed Caleb's hand, but he seemed not to even notice.

'Taking notes, are you, son?' Ralph asked.

'Wouldn't dream of it, sir.'

'Hmm. Shouldn't you be out there helping Damien do whatever it is he still has to do before this long night is over?'

Caleb smiled. 'Shouldn't you?'

'The father of the groom is obsolete. At least the father of the bride has a role, even if it is giving up his child.'

Ava's teeth clenched as she waited for him to acknowledge her in some way, but his stoic gaze didn't move.

This time Caleb squeezed her hand. The sense of warmth and safety he infused in her slowly returned. Making his sudden sideswipe all that much more perturbing.

'Poor fellow,' Caleb said. 'Then we'll just have to get this daughter of yours married off so you don't feel so obsolete. Though since she just so recently lost *another* boyfriend on the trail to becoming a sociologist, or a philosopher, or archaeologist, or whatever it is she's studying this week, I'm not sure what we are to do.'

Ava could do nothing but glare at Caleb. He smiled benignly at her as though she were the bride atop a wedding cake, but she saw the gleam in his eye.

She was *not* forgiven for what had happened in her bedroom. Far from it. Caleb had every intention of making her pay. For starting something? Or for stopping it?

The urge to kick him in the back of the knee and run was tempered by the lingering imprint of his lips upon her body.

'Oh, I don't mind not having a starring role in the play so much any more, Caleb,' her father said. 'It gives me more time to read the paper.'

'Then you are a luckier man than me.'

Pleasantries exhausted, Ralph Halliburton's eyes scooted back to Ava. 'I wasn't sure you'd made your flight.'

'It came in really early this morning and I knew you guys

would be really busy with the wedding and all so I went to a hotel.'

He nodded. Barely. 'Then I'll have someone sent to pick up your things and bring them back here.' It wasn't a question.

Ava thought about defying him. She really did. Anything to get a reaction from him. Any reaction. But in the end it only would have caused more friction and there was enough in the air to light a city. 'That would be great, Dad. Thanks.'

He smiled at Caleb, then reached out and shook the guy's hand. While he hadn't offered her a smile, a hug, a kiss on the cheek. Nothing. After ten years.

'See you kids later,' he said before walking away.

When it was just the two of them again Ava began to shake. 'What the hell was that all about? Marrying me off? Are you mad?'

'Mad? Me? Never. Happy about being the only one here who seems to have a clue *why* you're here? No, not that either.'

'And why's that?'

'Let's shelve this.'

'No,' she said, holding her ground. 'You've got something you're dying to say, so say it.'

'Fine. You've run away from your problems. Again. It's what you do.'

'Hardly.'

'My mistake. So you came back to quench the decade-long desire to have me again. I know I'm good, but that's given my ego a nice massage.'

'Get over yourself.'

'Maybe later. Right now I thought it best to keep your dad busy with a little inane conversation to give you time to come up with another reason that won't break your family's heart, is all. I was doing you a favour.'

'Well, don't do me any more.'

'Fine.'

'Fine.' Ava made to huff away, but it was only then that she realised they were still holding hands.

'Let me go, Caleb,' she said between gritted teeth.

He did so with such speed she rocked on the step.

'Sweetheart, I let you go a long time ago,' he said, giving her one last long look before he slid his hands into his trouser pockets, skipped down the last two steps and ambled away, whistling.

The bastard.

Ooh, she ached to… What? Hit him? Kick him? Humiliate him? Drag him back upstairs and finish what they'd started, once and for all?

'Ava!'

She closed her eyes tight and sent a few choice words to the gods for giving her such a perfect welcome home.

Then she turned towards the shrill voice with a smile plastered across her face. 'Yes, Aunt Gladys?'

Some time after three the next morning Ava sat on the frilly pink banquette below the window of her bedroom, wide awake.

Through the window she watched the wedding organisers pack while inside she relived the events of the past few weeks that had led her back home.

Taylor not thinking twice before taking the job on the Academic Review Committee. Coming home for the first time in almost ten years to a father who would barely look her in the eye. And, last but not least, the reckless and ultimately botched seduction of her brother's best friend in this very room.

She'd been looking for love in all the wrong places her whole life. Which was ridiculous. Her doctorate was in social anthropology; cultural development. Yet for an otherwise pretty bright woman she sure was eight kinds of dumb when it came to relationships with the men in her life.

Take Caleb. Once, years ago, he had given her everything he'd had to give on the one night when she'd so needed to have it. And tonight she'd thrown that back in his face, using him as she might have a gigolo, or a faceless man in a dark bar. As a means to feel desired again.

The moment the last marquee peg was packed away and the last van had driven off, the heavens finally opened, washing hard and fast buckets of rain over the Halliburtons' garden.

It was almost as though the clouds had crossed their legs until the coast was clear. Not so surprising. Nothing ever really went wrong for those who belonged on Stonnington Drive.

Her parents divorced, throwing her idyllic childhood into disarray. Yet now according to Damien they were best friends, which only served to throw her relationship barometer out of whack. Since she'd left, Caleb's life had gone from strength to strength. Even Marion Gilchrist, who must have been near sixty years old, had taken up pole-dancing and not yet broken a limb. And it never rained here on important days.

She wrapped her arms around her knees, her fingers catching on the frayed holes in the knees of her old, faded red flannel pyjama pants. And the raindrops sliding down her windowpane did little to mask the matching tears running down Ava's face, only proving she'd never really belonged here and never would.

CHAPTER SIX

SUNDAY morning Caleb got out of the car and tetchily slammed the door behind him. He stomped around to the Halliburtons' back entrance, knowing the terrace door would be open.

Sunday mornings in spring on Stonnington Drive meant tennis on the private courts, or golf at the private course that butted up against their backyards, or, for the really enthusiastic, laps of the pool. But in every house they meant a never-ending parade of food on the terrace from morning till night.

Caleb jogged up the back steps, grabbed a berry Danish from the fully laden table and headed through the open French doors and into the kitchen.

'Caleb, darling,' Rachel Halliburton, Ava and Damien's society queen of a mother, said as she passed by with an air kiss, her left hand grasping what looked very much like a Bloody Mary.

At eight in the morning that might have been shocking in any other house on any other street, but not here. His grumps dissipated a very little as he revelled in the idea that the rest of the world had no idea of the lifestyle they were missing.

'What are you doing here so bright and early?' she asked. 'Did you stay at your parents' house last night?'

'Ah, no. The king-sized bed in my apartment was enough to send me to my apartment last night. I'm here now for best-man duties. Damien insisted I attend the opening of the gifts. I'm hoping to pilfer a couple of the better ones to teach him a lesson.'

'Lovely. Lovely,' she said distractedly as she retied the lace on her new white tennis shoes.

Ralph Halliburton came in with a rolled-up broadsheet newspaper tucked under his arm. He patted his wife on her tennis-skirt-covered behind before making a beeline for the gigantic bubbling espresso machine.

'Not in front of the kids,' she cooed.

'Morning, Caleb,' Ralph said. 'What are you doing here so bright and early? Leave something behind yesterday?'

'Ah, no. I'm here to watch Damo and Chelsea unwrap a lot of useless electrical goods they don't want and don't need.'

'Excellent. Excellent,' Ralph said. 'Grab a coffee.'

'Maybe later. Can you point me the way to the groom?'

'Swimming, I do believe,' Rachel said. 'While his bride is outside playing with her wedding present.'

Caleb ambled over to the kitchen window, which looked out on the large garden. It was so green and clean nobody would have guessed they'd had two marquees and nearly four hundred people dining there the night before.

A squeak and a giggle drew his attention to the edge of the terrace. Chelsea's heels dug hard into the paving, her blonde pony-tail wagging madly as she held tight to a length of hot-pink rope in both hands, while a tiny black and white fox terrier puppy had the other caught between its teeth. The puppy growled with as much vigour as a puppy could while Chelsea laughed. And laughed and laughed.

The only word Caleb could use to describe his best friend's bride in that moment was *happy*. He realised with some chagrin that that word was making rather a lot of appearances on his radar of late.

Chelsea glanced up, blew her fringe from her eyes, and gave him a big wave. He saluted back, then pointed to where the puppy was making a run for the back steps. She laughed some more, then took off after it.

Caleb realised that, despite having to be there at such a hideous hour, there was no way he could begrudge his friend a moment of the life he'd have with the woman, insidiously happy as she was.

He turned back to face the kitchen at large. 'Either Damo bought Chelsea a dog or a piece of pink rope. Which is it?'

'A dog, I tell you,' Rachel said. 'We tried to convince him to buy her a new car so she would stop having to drive that odd pink business van of hers around the place. But no. Ralph, how did we raise a son with such whack priorities?'

'How indeed?' Ralph said, leaning in to kiss his ex-wife on the end of the nose. Then he took his newspaper, his fresh coffee and himself outside, while Rachel mooned after him until he was out of sight.

His feet itching to get moving, get gone, or get anywhere but around all this happy, smiley coupledom, Caleb was about to scoot out to the pool when Ava came clumping down the stairs.

His feet stayed put and instead he slowly sank back against the kitchen bench.

She was dressed like uni students everywhere. Faded jeans frayed at the cuffs, red sneakers, a baby-blue zipped-up track-suit top, hair pulled back into a messy bun atop her head, glasses perched on the end of her nose.

The dog-eared novel tucked under her arm was pure Ava. She never went anywhere without one as a kid. Boy, that brought back a flood of memories. Nice ones. Sweet ones.

Ones that threatened to negate the healthy antagonism he'd built up the evening before.

She still wore the leather strap, which he now knew held the locket he'd once given her. What he didn't know was if the picture inside it had been long since changed. They hadn't quite gone far enough the night before for him to find out.

Wrong, he corrected himself. They'd gone too far before her motives had come into the light. She'd been jilted and was looking for comfort. He wasn't comfort guy. The end.

So why did the mere sight of her have him feeling like a tightly coiled spring?

'Morning, Avocado,' he called out when she looked as though she might head right on out of the kitchen without even noticing he was there.

She looked up and upon seeing him faltered on the next to last step, catching herself on the stair rail at the last second.

It took a couple of moments for her to collect her breath before she frowned like a champion and shuffled groggily past him.

'My, my,' he said. 'Don't we look tired? Still on Boston time? Or did your conscience keep you up all night?'

'Bite me.'

'Ava, darling,' Rachel said, 'go upstairs and put something more appropriate on, please. We have company.'

Ava looked pointedly around the room. 'I don't see any company.'

'What am I?' Calcb asked. 'Chopped liver?'

'That would be insulting to chopped liver,' she said beneath her breath. 'Why are you here anyway? Too lazy to find another family to bug?'

Caleb laughed at the third Halliburton to question him with the exact same words in as many minutes. 'You're your parents' daughter, that's for sure.'

Ava crossed her arms and glared daggers at him. 'You take that back!'

Caleb glanced at Rachel, who was swanning around the kitchen with white iPod cords dangling from her ears, Totally oblivious, as she had always been when it came to her daughter.

He scratched the back of his head as he explained, 'You all asked the exact same…oh, never mind. I'm here because Damien asked me to help take the gifts back to his and Chelsea's new house.'

He turned towards the coffee machine, grabbed a mug and said under his breath, 'Brat.'

The slap of book against granite kitchen bench-top reverberated through his arm.

'What did you just call me?'

He took his sweet time to finish pouring, added a gulp of cream, then pushed the mug towards her.

Her half-hearted, 'Thank you,' got him off the hook.

As Caleb poured his own strong black coffee Damien came into the room with wet hair and a damp towel slung over his shoulder. 'Morning, all.'

A chorus of hellos echoed around the room. His mother fixed his hair, his father waved with his newspaper from the terrace, and Ava watched it all with a knotted brow.

She glanced back at Caleb, saw he was watching her, then her frown turned to a glare.

He laughed, she frowned all the more, then huffed over to the fridge. She stuck her head inside, her right knee kicked out sideways and her right foot resting snugly against her calf.

All that pose did was pull her jeans tight across her buttocks. From behind she still looked a nubile nineteen. Lean, curvy, and fit as a fiddle. Caleb couldn't have dragged his eyes away for all the coffee in Brazil.

Then she pulled her hair from its elastic band and shook it out, scratching her fingers through her scalp until her hair fell in long, sexy, messy waves. He would have put money on the fact that she had no idea she was doing it. And he would have bet his life savings on the fact that she was doing it because she subconsciously wanted to look good for him.

It seemed he wasn't the only one left feeling as if the night before was unfinished business.

He settled thoughtfully against the bench and took a sip of coffee. The hot drink scorched a layer off the top of his tongue. He glanced skyward and muttered a soft curse at whoever up there might be listening.

She finally came out of the fridge with a piece of pizza that looked as if it had seen better days.

'Don't tell me you've been living on stale pizza for the past ten years,' he said.

'Fine,' she said through a mouthful of just that as she turned and pinned him with a fierce stare. 'I won't tell you that.'

'Stale pizza ain't cheap. How could a poor student afford to live so well, I do wonder?'

She ambled back over to her coffee and leant against the counter beside him, close enough that the back of his neck bristled. He was sure he'd know if she was in the room even with his eyes closed, he was so well tuned to her.

When she didn't deign to answer Caleb filled in the blanks himself. 'Perhaps you work in the college bookstore? Pull beer at an off-campus bar for tips? Sleep on friends' floors and raid their cupboards when everyone else is asleep? Aah, no. I'd forgotten about Daddy's trust fund.'

Her initial verbal response post-swallowing was less than ladylike. Then, 'Look who's talking. I never knew a guy so eager to get to twenty-five so that he could take the money and run. What was the plan again? Blow it all on black at the casino? No, you were going to buy a boat and cruise the Caribbean making friends with the local girls until the dough ran out. How did that work out for you?'

Caleb had forgotten he'd ever said that. Likely he'd been showing off, making noise, trying to get attention from the bright, pretty girl. However, he gave her a slow smile as he said, 'Who says my life plan has changed any?'

Antagonism radiated from her like a spicy perfume. But rather than make Caleb realise he'd dodged a bullet the night before, the intensity of her reaction to him was infectious.

It made him want to taste more of that soft, sweet skin. To kiss her until her knees melted, until she could scarce draw breath. Until she could no longer remember the name of the fool back in Boston who had jilted her, thus sending her into his arms in the first place.

That was what it might well take to get her well and truly out of his system once and for all.

His smile was forbidding. 'Now that we've established my life is hunky-dory, I think we really should be shining the spotlight onto yours,' he said. 'Last night didn't you mention something about a review?'

Ava's mouth shot open but Damien chimed in before she could tell Caleb exactly what he could do with his spotlight.

'Damn, you two are painful. And since I know you'd both rather push each other's buttons far more than you'd like to actually answer a simple question… Ava, Caleb used his trust-fund money to help me buy the business. Without him, then and now, Keppler, Jones and Morgenstern would be another pesky upstart two-man operation rather than the company every other trading company wants to be.'

Caleb shifted on the spot, not all that comfortable being seen as responsible. It hardly did his mad, bad and danger-ous-to-know image any good.

Ava's mouth snapped shut, and when she looked back at him her expression had changed. She looked at him differently. As if maybe she ought not to have sniped at him after all.

His skin contracted agreeably. The night before hadn't been an anomaly. He wondered if she had any idea that sniping was the only thing staving off the kissing.

'And, Caleb,' Damien said with a warning tone that Caleb could not mistake.

'Yes, Damien,' he said, loading the two words with as much indolence as he could.

Damien simply didn't pay him any heed. 'Apart from the numerous scholarships she's earned, Ava tutors and guest lectures at universities around the States. She's written numerous articles about human behaviour for magazines including a couple of hilarious ones for *The New Yorker*. She has recently become a darling of the business conference circuit. And she lives on campus in order to save money. She does all right.' Damien reached out and ran a hard hand over Ava's hair, mussing it up even further.

She quickly flattened it down and glanced at Caleb from beneath her fringe. While Caleb held tight to his coffee and wondered if she had any idea that he was itching to run his hands through those sexy waves himself.

He said, 'You must be so proud of your little flag bearer for the great unwashed.'

Damien rolled his eyes. 'Why I ever thought that getting the two of you together again would take me back to the fun, fabulous days of our youth I have no idea. Now I remember you were always at each other's throats. I must have blocked that part out.'

He shook his head and took up Ava's place standing at the open fridge.

Having finished her pizza, Ava twisted to pick up her

coffee. Her jacket tipped forward ever so slightly, but just enough Caleb caught a hint of white lace bra. He gritted his teeth and swallowed. Who knew having one more layer between them than they did the night before would prove to be an even bigger turn-on?

He shifted closer. She noticed and frowned. But she didn't move away.

'I had no idea you'd become so conscientious,' she said.

'Sure. And I spend my Saturday nights helping little old ladies across the street too,' Caleb said. 'Now I don't think we actually sorted out the subject of your trust fund…'

'I gave it up.' She took a slow sip of her coffee, those big blue eyes of hers just waiting for his reaction.

Caleb realised he must have looked like a fish out of water, his mouth dropped open so fast. He ran a finger over the edge of his mouth before saying, 'Right, and I've been contemplating the priesthood.'

'Do you want me to take you upstairs and show you? The paperwork is collecting dust in my bedside drawer as we speak.'

She took a step away from him.

Caleb snaked a hand out and grabbed her wrist. 'You want me to come up to your room with you? Right now? Just the two of us?'

Ava's cheeks turned beautifully pink and her gaze shot from her wrist to her brother. Damien was whistling beneath his breath and pretending he hadn't heard a thing. But Caleb was on the right angle to see the guy was smiling.

'No,' Ava said. 'I don't. How about I fax them to you later when you've left? When will that be, exactly?'

He slowly let her go, smiling as she rubbed the spot where he'd held her, as though trying to erase his touch.

'No need,' he said. 'I can tell by the clothes on your back you're obviously skint.'

'And you're insufferable,' Ava said.

'Nah,' Caleb said, 'I'm lovely. My mother told me so every day until I moved out. Heck, that's why I moved out.'

Damien's shoulders began to shake. He was enjoying this. Mostly because he knew way too much for Caleb's comfort. Caleb wanted very much to get his friend in a headlock until he cried mercy. Even then he might think long and hard before letting the pain come to an end.

Caleb was pretty sure Damien wouldn't be smiling if he knew while he'd been feeding cake to his bride, the two of them had been up to all kinds of no good upstairs. In fact if Damien knew the kinds of no good Caleb was yet contemplating perpetrating on his sister he might be the one in danger of gross pain.

He'd even dreamt of ways to teach her lessons, in great detail. Until his stupid alarm had woken him so that he could come here and ooh and aah over all the wedding gifts.

'Remind me never to get married,' he said beneath his breath.

This time Ava heard him loud and clear. 'Never get married. For the sake of the human race, please never get married.'

Before Caleb had the chance to come back with some pithy remark Chelsea came bounding inside with the puppy in her arms.

Thank God, Ava thought. The more people in the room to take her focus off Caleb, the better.

She had to admit he looked good today. If at all possible, even better than he had in his tuxedo the night before. Loose jeans clung to his narrow hips, a navy V-necked jumper with a red T-shirt underneath did very little to hide the hard planes beneath, and the lightweight pale grey blazer he wore over the top just dripped money. His hair was slightly more mussed and his stubble more grown in. He really was just about the most naturally gorgeous guy she'd ever known. If only he didn't know it.

He looked up and caught her staring. And he didn't look away. The air between them crackled and she was hit with a sense memory of his taste, his touch, and the ease with which she'd gone from seductress to putty in his hands.

She'd gone to him for validation. What she'd found was trouble.

Chelsea's dramatic sigh turned everyone to the kitchen door to find her shucking off her grass-covered shoes. Her cheeks were pink from exertion and delight. She jogged up to Damien and kissed him full on the mouth. He wrapped an arm about her waist and when she was about to pull away he tucked her in close and continued the kiss for a second or two longer. That was all. But it was enough for all of Chelsea's energy to leech out of her as she quite simply sank against him.

Ava leant her elbows on the kitchen bench and just watched them.

She'd never doubted her mother and father would be contented with one another their whole lives, and their relationship had fallen apart. The fact that it had slowly been rebuilt from the ashes didn't negate the dark years in between. She hoped against hope that her brother would have greater luck.

There was only one species she had ever found in her extensive studies on the subject that was absolutely monogamous. In the deepest sea, the tiny male anglerfish found the scent trail of a female, followed her, bit her and hung on. Their skins literally fused, their bodies grew together and they mated for life. She'd always thought it was in its own way terribly romantic.

Her brother gave his bride a kiss on the end of her nose and she beamed up at him. Ava hoped that it wouldn't take something as painful as the fusing of skins for them to last.

If two such substantial people couldn't make it, what hope would she ever have?

Ava couldn't help it. She casually tipped her head just enough so that she could glance at Caleb.

She needn't have bothered with the finessing. He wasn't hiding the fact that his eyes were all for her.

His left hand covered his mouth, his pointer finger ran slowly, hypnotically, across his bottom lip. He blinked. Slowly. And she knew without a doubt he was thinking about kissing her. And so much more.

She looked away before he could see how much she wanted to kiss him right back.

She felt him sink back against the bench, his elbow rested inches from hers. His warmth infused her as fast as if he'd set her sleeve on fire.

His little finger reached out and ran up and down the side of her hand. Her eyes fluttered closed. She'd never known such simple pleasure in her life. What she did know was that she'd been kidding herself thinking the night before might be some kind of cure-all. If anything she felt even more at sea than she had been before.

'Knock, knock.'

Ava jumped so high at the sudden loud voice from the terrace she pulled a muscle in her side. She moved away from Caleb, glancing at him briefly, but long enough to see he was grinning. Then with a hand pressing against her waist she turned to find a brunette with curls and an oversized handbag covered in flamingos standing in the doorway.

'Morning, sis,' Chelsea said, waving at the woman with her puppy's paw.

Damien turned out of his wife's embrace but still kept an arm about her waist. 'Has everyone eaten?'

Chelsea gave him the puppy, then raced to the fridge, but

she was in and out in half a second. 'Give me three minutes to make a couple of boiled eggs, then I'm all yours.'

'Ah-h-h, too late, Mrs Halliburton, that's what the vows and rings and guests and cake and DJ and stuff was all about last night.'

Chelsea slapped a hand to her head. 'Right. I keep forgetting.'

'Oh, how beloved you make me feel. Now we're all here we should get this show on the road. I for one can't wait to see how many Royal Doulton tea sets our nearest and dearest think two people need.'

He held an arm towards the double swing doors leading to the living room. Ralph and Rachel meandered on through. Chelsea's sister waited for Caleb and slung an arm through his elbow and began chatting to him as if they were long-lost friends.

Ava waited for him to send her a look, of explanation or grief, an inclusive smile or a glance that said he'd rather it were her arm through his elbow. But she got nothing.

Her head hurt. Her cheeks felt hot. Her hands felt cold. Her stomach felt tight. Her feet felt numb. She wondered if anyone would believe her if she begged off with a sudden case of the flu.

CHAPTER SEVEN

'I'M SO glad you were able to make it,' Chelsea said.

Ava turned to find her sister-in-law at the stove with a saucepan full of enough water to boil eggs to feed the household twice over.

She opened her mouth to say so, then decided being a bossy boots wasn't the best way to start a relationship with her only sister-in-law. 'Oh, well, my pleasure.'

'It's all Damien talked about the last days leading up to the wedding. I don't think he would have had as good a time had you not been able to get away.'

'I don't know about that. From what I've seen he only has eyes for you.'

Chelsea let go an exaggerated sigh. 'Do you have any idea how nice that is?'

'What, me? Well, no. Not so much. Unfortunately.'

'Mmm,' Chelsea said. 'Are you quite sure?'

Without her meaning them to, Ava's eyes shot to the now still swing doors leading to the living room. There was a man behind those doors who she'd caught staring her way more often than not. But the only reason she knew that was because she hadn't been able to stop staring at him.

She glanced back at Chelsea, who was looking that way too, before her gaze swung back to Ava.

'Would you like an egg?' Chelsea asked, an all too knowing half-smile on her face.

'No. No, thanks. All filled up on stale pizza. A student's staple meal,' Ava said. And then after a moment of panic she added, 'Hard-boiled eggs will spin on a flat surface. Uncooked or soft-boiled eggs will not.'

'I did not know that.' She smiled, her soft brown eyes telling Ava what politeness would not. That she was there, a friend. Happy to talk if she needed it. And that Damien had obviously told her about the situation with Taylor.

But Ava had never had a sister. She'd never even had a really close girlfriend. She'd grown up with boys, then concentrated so hard on her studies through high school then had moved from subject to subject, course to course, college to college, boyfriend to boyfriend, country to country, ever since.

Maybe talking would have been a sensible problem-solving alternative to throwing herself at Caleb. But it was a tad late for all that.

She pointed a thumb towards the living room as she backed away. 'I'd better go in there. In case he's wondering where I am. Damien, I mean.'

Chelsea smiled and nodded.

Ava grabbed *Love in the Time of Cholera* off the kitchen bench and backed away.

Once in the lounge, Ava slid her book beside her and sat on the edge of the couch, tucking her feet beneath her meditation-style.

Caleb leant against the mantle laughing with Damien. When her brother realised Chelsea still hadn't joined them he patted Caleb on the arm and went to find her.

Caleb pushed away from the mantle and headed towards the lounge. She fully expected him to take the farthest point in the room so that he could have prime position from which to toss conversational grenades at her without fear of getting hit back, but instead he veered past the mammoth teak coffee table and sat on the long couch beside her.

She turned to glare at him instead, but he was watching some vague point in the distance with a small serene smile on his face. Eventually he turned to her and smiled as though he'd only just realised she was even there.

Was he serious? Barely two minutes earlier he'd been seducing her with little more than his little finger.

She gritted her teeth and motioned to the other end of the long couch with her chin.

His brow furrowed.

She motioned again, this time raising her eyebrows in the general direction of 'as far away as possible'.

He mouthed, Are you okay?

Rather than lose it at him, she looked away. Her mum was pulling up an oversized ottoman so as to be closest to the gifts piled in the corner of the room. Her dad took his place on his usual wing chair.

Caleb poked her in the leg.

She glowered at him.

He grinned and let his hand linger by her thigh. Half of her wanted him to leave it there, tantalising her, the other half wanted to snap it in two.

She wondered how on earth she could tell him to shove over without making a complete scene. But if she moved her chin again she feared she might dislocate something.

By the time that thought was thought it was too late. Chelsea's sister Kensey sat on Caleb's right and they were trapped. He moved closer to her on the pretence he was giving Kensey more room. Ava knew he was merely taking every opportunity possible to punish her.

Meaning she would have to spend the next hour drinking

in the faint scent of Safari aftershave Caleb had always worn.
And feeling the shuffle of his jeans against hers every time
he leaned forward to take a sip of his coffee.

'Didn't think you had it in you to drag yourself here so
early, Caleb,' Kensey said, her voice bright and cheerful.

'Lovely to see you again, Mrs Hurley.'

'So you remembered I'm married this time?'

'How could I not? I have caffeine trickling into my system,
the sun is shining and you're no longer wearing hot-pink taffeta.
My brain is able to function better under these circumstances.'

Ava scoffed loudly. Then regretted it the second she felt
Kensey lean forward. She fought against the urge to screw up
her face and instead turned into the conversation.

'Hi there. I don't think we met yesterday…' Kensey began.

Ava reached across Caleb and held out her hand. 'I'm Ava,
Damien's sister.'

When she leant back, Caleb's arm was resting along the
back of the couch behind her. Even though she knew she'd
end up with a terrible neck ache she leant forward just enough
they weren't touching.

'I didn't think you could come,' Kensey said. 'Something
about your uni professor keeping you strapped to your desk.'

This time it was Caleb's turn to scoff.

Kensey smiled, then frowned. 'I feel like I keep stepping
into conversational minefields without knowing it.'

'Not at all,' Ava insisted as she leant back suddenly, trapping
Caleb's wandering hand between her shoulder blades and the
couch. His sharp intake of breath was most satisfying.

And then he, oh, so slowly, began manipulating his hand until
it flipped and tucked along the back of her neck, beneath her hair.
And then he began to stroke, soft, leisurely, heavenly strokes.

'This guy ever conveniently forget you were married too?'
Kensey asked.

'Ah, no,' Ava said, her voice croaky. She cleared her throat. 'Not married.'

'But he must have hit on you, right? He's so bad, and you're an utter doll. Why didn't Chelsea tell me you were such a doll?'

'Maybe she doesn't think I'm a doll.'

'How could she not?' Caleb interjected, but was promptly ignored by both women. Or ignored by Ava as much as he could be while he had his fingers curled deliciously hard within her hair.

'I wonder if he ever hit on Chelsea?' Kensey said, eyes bright at the thought. 'She never said, but that doesn't mean it didn't happen. Far too discreet, my sister.'

'Wouldn't surprise me,' Ava said, getting into the swing of things, and trying her best to disregard the warmth tingling down her back and making her feel as if she were floating off the couch. 'He always was the brazen type.'

'If I sat back with a napkin over my eyes and had a little nap you guys could just carry on without me, I take it,' Caleb said.

'Gladly,' Kensey and Ava said at the same time.

Kensey grinned. While Ava bit her bottom lip to stop from groaning when Caleb started massaging her neck.

'There's too many women in this family now, Ralph,' Caleb called loudly across to Ava's dad.

He looked up from his newspaper with a slightly bewildered expression.

Caleb poked his spare thumb at each of the brunettes bookending him and said, 'Suddenly the women in this family outnumber us. When did that happen?'

'Complain about it all you like, Caleb, my boy, but I'm afraid I won't be joining the naysayers. The more women the better has long since been my motto.'

Caleb's mouth turned down and he nodded as his gaze flittered briefly to Kensey. Then he turned to look Ava dead in the eye. 'Good point, Ralph. What was I thinking?'

Ava breathed deep through her nose and sniffed in a compelling waft of that drinkable aftershave. Her heart rate sped to a gallop as his hot hazel gaze pinned her to the back of the chair. If he wasn't reliving every moment in her arms the night before then she was more clueless than even she imagined she was.

'Oh, yeah,' he said, staring at her far longer than was in any way civilised. 'I remember what I was thinking. They may smell great and be pretty to look at, but they did have to steal one of our ribs to get here.'

Her father's laughter echoed across the room. That sound was the only thing that could have dragged Ava's eyes from Caleb's gaze. Her dad's dark blue eyes were twinkling. Ava felt a smile building inside her seeing her father content. It had been so long…

The simple lazy hazy days of her childhood, when her dad taught her how to ride a bike along the path by the golf course. When they and the Gilchrists had spent every Melbourne winter water-skiing in Belize and every Melbourne summer snow skiing in Aspen. Her life had been simple then. Safe. Happy. Until the day the fighting had started and everything she'd ever known had begun to crumble at her young feet.

She blinked and realised her father was looking at her, a small crease between his bright blue eyes.

Terrified of doing or saying something that would wipe that smile off his face, Ava did that thing people did when caught staring: she shifted her gaze an inch to the left, then slowly let it trail away.

'Get more than one man in a room and they all revert back to childhood,' Kensey said. 'I'd know, I have four. Kids, not men. So do you have kids, Ava?'

'Ah, no.'

'A fella?'

Caleb snorted loud enough that Ava jumped and his fingers tangled in her hair, tugged, and hurt. Her eyes watered, but she couldn't do anything about it because then everyone would know what he'd been doing to her all along.

Kensey's smile merely grew wider. 'You two are all about the in jokes, I see. Would you prefer I sit somewhere else?'

Ava said, 'I'd prefer he sit somewhere else.'

'Ooh,' Kensey said, eyes darting from one to the other. 'It's like that, is it?'

'It's not like anything. We're not like anything,' Ava shot back, quickly lifting her hair from the back of her neck and sitting forward, the second Caleb dropped his guard.

Nevertheless Kensey tapped the side of her nose as though she knew better.

'So where is your husband this fine morning?' Caleb asked, casually pulling his hand back to rest beside him on the couch.

Ava could have kissed him for getting her off the hook. Well, not kissed him. Punched his shoulder in camaraderie. Shaken his hand…

'Babysitting,' Kensey said. 'His first day alone with our newborn and the other three. If I don't go home to the lot of them hyped up on sugar then I'll eat my foot. So, Caleb, no kids for you either?'

'Not that he knows of,' Ava muttered.

Caleb slapped his hand down on her thigh. It stung and set her blood racing so fast through her veins she only hoped her face didn't turn bright pink.

'How could I,' Caleb asked, 'when the woman of my dreams won't do me the honour of incubating them for me? Don't you think our genes would make one beautiful baby? Ava? Honey bunny?''

She gritted her teeth to stop from groaning, then said, 'Keep your hands off my genes, Caleb Gilchrist.'

'Yeah,' he said, pulling his hand away and wiping it on his own jeans. 'I guess it would be hard for us to raise a family living on a friend's floor and eating stale pizza. I hereby withdraw my offer to father your children. So stop asking me.'

Ava lifted her leg to her chest, crossed her arms over it, getting as far away from the guy as possible, and said, 'Oh, shut up.'

'Ava,' her father chastised from his chair.

'He started it.'

'She made me,' Caleb shot right on back.

'Get a room,' Kensey added with a grin, and that shut the both of them up more than any other three words could have.

'Play nice, you two,' Damien said as he and Chelsea entered the room, arms around one another, bodies tucked tight, faces lit by the brightest smiles two people could have.

Ava somehow managed to rein herself in before she gave in to the desperate desire to poke her tongue out at her big brother. Mostly because she was certain Caleb would use it as a way to make her feel even more warm and fidgety than she already did.

An hour later only a tenth of the presents had been opened and they had all had too much coffee, too much left-over wedding cake and were all feeling a tad silly.

Kensey had been put in charge of folding the wrapping paper. Ava had no idea why as her mother would never deign to reuse any such thing. But it also meant that she and Caleb now had the couch to themselves.

The chair beneath Ava's bottom lifted as Caleb leaned towards her. He came so close she would have leant away if not for the high arm of the chair digging into her ribs. So instead she was left looking deep into a pair of cheeky hazel eyes that were flashing with the thrill of adventure.

Adventure she was certain by that stage had everything to do with her and the couch.

'Caleb…' she warned under her breath.

He reached over her and threw a couple of gift cards he'd been pretending to be interested in into the pile in her lap. 'I'm going stir crazy here.'

'Well, tough. You're the best man—this is your duty.'

'Who are you to talk of duty, Ms Prodigal Daughter?'

She shot him her dirtiest look complete with curled lip. Caleb reached up, put a finger over her mouth to wipe the look away. She grabbed his hand, held it tight in her lap then quickly looked out over the crowd to make sure nobody noticed. Thankfully everyone was watching Chelsea hold up a crystal bowl to the light, much more excited about the fact that her puppy was chasing the rainbow prisms the bowl was creating on the walls than the extravagant label dangling noticeably off the side.

Ava laughed despite herself and felt a little happy thrill shoot down her centre that her brother had found himself such a truly down-to-earth bride. If Chelsea didn't bring the Halliburton household down a peg or two nobody could.

A sudden tickle of hair against her neck had her whipping her attention back to Caleb, who was brushing her hair from her shoulder.

'Are you trying to drive me crazy?'

'Not at all. You had a…thing on your neck. I was just brushing it off.'

He continued staring at the point where her neck met her shoulder and the happy thrill she'd felt for Damien had nothing on the flash of energy that poured through her every vein at the look in Caleb's eyes.

'A thing?' she repeated, her voice giveaway deep.

His gaze slowly meandered up her neck to her face and she felt every centimetre his gaze touched heat from the inside out.

When his eyes met hers they were dark. Shadowed. 'Can we please—?'

'I like the look of this one,' Chelsea called out as she picked up a foot long silver box and shook it.

Caleb breathed out hard through his nose and his frustration seeped into Ava until she had to wiggle her toes to lose some of the excess energy coursing through her.

'Ooh, what if it's those new Versace salad servers?' Rachel said, eyes bright.

'No, I recognise the paper,' Kensey said. 'I think it's something from that fancy candle place at Chadstone.'

By this stage even Ralph had put down his newspaper and was staring at the box as though he could see through it. 'I'm thinking…sterling silver scroll container in which to put your wedding certificate.'

Everyone in the room oohed at Ralph's inspired guess. He pinked a bit about the ears. 'My mother gave Rachel and me one for our wedding,' he explained.

'How much will you pay me to shout out the obvious?' Caleb murmured into her ear. 'The looks on your parents' faces would be a treat.'

She laughed through her nose. It *was* just the right shape for it to have come from an adult supply shop. 'Please, this morning has been the most pleasant time I've spent with my family as long as I can remember. Don't ruin it by throwing a vibrator into the mix.'

'Possible vibrator,' he said, his voice a mite louder.

She turned to glare at him to find he was close enough she could make out every speck of stubble on his fabulous jaw. She swallowed as circumspectly as possible before saying, 'I'll give you five bucks not to say it and ten if you'll keep your mouth shut for the rest of the day.'

He smiled so wide she was privy to every perfect tooth, and

was forced to remember just what he could do with them when given half a chance. She needed to swallow again.

'Ten, eh?' he said. 'Tempting. But I do think the offer needs a little sweetening.'

She looked back into his eyes, hoping for reprieve, but instead found them brimming with so much unsuppressed hunger her throat squeezed shut. She managed to choke out, 'Pretty please with sugar on top?'

'Mmm.' His deep voice rumbled down her spine. 'Not exactly the kind of sweetening I had in mind.'

'What goes on in your mind is a mystery to all mankind.'

She glanced back to the proceedings, lest he see in her eyes how much he was getting to her and how much she was enjoying just being herself. With him. It was so easy.

'Then how about a hint?' he offered.

'Ah, not necessary.' The thought of Caleb spelling out in any kind of detail that which he thought tempting and sweet that she could supply made her knees itch. 'I've decided to rescind the offer altogether.'

'Caleb,' Chelsea called out, her hand ready to tear the paper, 'what do you think it is?'

He opened his mouth, took in a deep breath.

'Don't.' Ava clamped down on his hand, which she realised she still held in her lap.

He closed his fingers over hers before she could let him go, thought for a few seconds, then said, 'I'm going with fridge freezer. No ice-maker included, unfortunately. Cheapskates.'

Everyone laughed appreciatively.

Ava let go of the breath she'd been holding. And at the same time gave up and let go of her resolution to appear unaffected. Being affected felt too good. Indulging couldn't hurt. She turned her hand until it fitted snug in his, their fingers intertwined.

'You owe me,' he rumbled.

Ava decided it best not to ask how much.

Chelsea tore open the package and inside was a marble statuette of a naked woman writhing around a tree trunk.

Kensey peeled the card from the discarded wrapping. She opened it and read, 'From Aunt Gladys.'

Everyone nodded in understanding. Everyone bar Ava, who was busily biting her lip as the back of Caleb's hand ran up and down her zipper.

'Next!' Damien said from his position on the far couch where he had a good view of his wife having too much fun opening all the presents.

Ava shifted position, lest Caleb go a centimetre further. Their hands fell apart. But at some stage she and Caleb had come to be sitting so close she was all but leaning against him. If this didn't end and soon she was going to end up sitting on his lap and there'd be no hiding their games from her family then.

'Open the little one,' Ava said, pointing to a small black box. 'It's from me.'

Chelsea picked it up, held it to her ear and shook it.

'It's a matchbox collection,' Caleb muttered near her ear.

She waved a hand at him to shoosh him as she watched Chelsea unpick the sticky tape.

'No? Then it's a pack of cards.'

'Will you keep it down, please?'

'Just tell me now if you made it yourself so I don't accidentally say something stupid when all is revealed.'

'There's nothing I could say to stop you.'

'The first step is admitting it,' he whispered, and she had to close her eyes to stop from screaming, 'though, to put you out of your misery, my final guess is…matching harmonicas.'

All shooshing from Ava ceased as she turned to glare at Caleb.

There came a final ripping of paper and a slide of cardboard, then Chelsea's bewildered voice said, 'It's a pair of harmonicas.'

'Get out of here!' Damien said, leaping out of his chair and grabbing them out of her hands to inspect them.

But Ava was staring at Caleb, gob smacked. And his gob seemed smacked right back.

'You cannot be serious,' he said.

At the same time she said, 'How did you possibly know?'

She felt the rumble of his laughter shake against her side. She frowned. 'Don't you dare laugh at me, Caleb Gilchrist. You know how much I hate it.'

'Well, then, lucky for both of us I'm not laughing at you, I'm laughing near you. A harmonica? Twice over. Are they meant to serenade one another on their honeymoon?'

'The harmonica is the world's best-selling instrument. And look!'

She pointed at her brother, who was already playing with it. And he was holding Chelsea's to her mouth and she was laughing at the horrible cacophony of sounds their duet produced.

'And look,' she whispered, placing a soft hand on Caleb's knee and angling her chin towards her father who was now on the edge of his seat.

'Well, I'll be,' Ralph said, watching his son with delight written across his face. 'A mouth harp. I used to have one of those darned things years ago. Was a fine player in my day. I wonder what happened to it.'

Ava knew.

She and Damien had loved it when their dad used to bring it out late at night and played beautiful sad songs by the firelight. But it had been swept away, out of sight, out of mind, during the dark years of The Divorce, just as she had been.

NO POSTAGE
NECESSARY
IF MAILED
IN THE
UNITED STATES

BUSINESS REPLY MAIL

FIRST-CLASS MAIL   PERMIT NO. 717   BUFFALO, NY

POSTAGE WILL BE PAID BY ADDRESSEE

Harlequin Reader Service
3010 WALDEN AVENUE
PO BOX 1867
BUFFALO NY 14240-9952

Get FREE MERCHANDISE!

CROSSWORD GAME

Scratch the
gold area on this
Crossword Game
to see
what you're
getting... **FREE!**

306 HDL ESXQ   106 HDL ESJF

FIRST NAME   LAST NAME

ADDRESS

APT. #   CITY

STATE/PROV.   ZIP/POSTAL CODE

Order online at:
www.try2free.com

Damien looked her way with a slight gleam to his eyes. He held her gift up in salute. She felt her throat catch.

'What do you know?' Caleb said.

'A heck of a lot more than you've given me credit for, my friend,' Ava said as she crossed her arms and sank back into the couch, vindicated. And with a lightness about her that she hadn't felt in days. Weeks. Months. Years. As if the world around her was finally beginning to make sense again.

'Come on, kids,' Rachel said when the production line had ground to a halt for too long. 'Next gift, please.'

The next box Chelsea chose was a similar shape to the naked lady statue, only bigger and wrapped in flesh-coloured paper.

Ava tipped her face into her open palm. She felt Caleb shaking with laughter beside her.

CHAPTER EIGHT

SOME time after midday Caleb stood, stretched his arms over his head and twisted his back to loosen up while the others filtered from the room. 'I've been sitting in that damn couch so long I'm afraid my backside shape will never be the same again.'

Kensey tilted her head to have a look. 'Looks fine to me.'

Caleb smiled and looked to Ava, who was staring hard at his backside with a small frown on her face. 'Care to give your opinion?'

She held her book to her chest and blinked. 'I'm not checking out your backside and I'm certainly not grading you on it.'

He let his arms drop. 'You don't need to. I'm onto you.'

With that he walked back into the kitchen, knowing she couldn't help but follow.

'You're onto me how?' she asked as she jogged up behind him.

'You couldn't keep your eyes off me in there.'

'Excuse me! My eyes were all for the lovely shiny presents.'

'Of course they were,' he said as he mingled with her family.

'You're one to talk,' she said, having to get really close so her voice wouldn't carry. 'You couldn't keep your hands off me.'

'You're right,' he said. 'I couldn't. In fact I'm struggling not to touch you right now.'

She snapped her mouth shut and looked like a firecracker ready to pop. Caleb had every intention of being there when she went off.

He grabbed a mini-focaccia from the batch the Halliburtons' cook had whipped up, popped it in his mouth and pretended to pay attention to Damien and Chelsea's rundown on their honeymoon plans.

All the while he was thinking of how he could get Ava alone. And as far as he could tell Ava wasn't taking the hint.

She always had been book smart far more than street smart. Which was a hazard in itself. Caleb found that there was something immeasurably seductive about a clever woman. The quick wit, the utter absorption in whatever held her fancy, a whole world going on behind those sexy glasses.

It was time to get to the point.

'Do you want to get out of here?' he murmured.

The flare in her eyes gave her away before she said, 'I'm not sure I can.'

She glanced over to her parents, who were starting to head off into their separate zones. Her mother was limbering up and her father had found yet another newspaper to read. 'I probably should stay and—'

'Ava, honey,' Rachel called out, unaware as always of anything else going on around her, 'stand up straight or your boobs will hit your navel before you're forty.'

Caleb lost it. He laughed so loud even Rachel stopped jogging on the spot and stared at him.

When he'd collected himself he smiled at Ava and lifted an eyebrow.

'Get me out of here,' she begged.

'Done. Damo,' he said, 'there's nothing more you need us for imminently?'

Damien dragged his eyes away from his bride to stare through Caleb as his words infiltrated. 'Ah, no. Not imminently.'

'Excellent. Rachel, you don't mind me stealing your precious daughter away, do you?'

Rachel flapped a hand at him. 'Not in the least. Go, go.'

'Great.'

Caleb grabbed Ava's hand and headed to the terrace. He caught Damien's eye on the way out and what he saw in his best friend's eye wasn't comforting. It wasn't even all that friendly. But he'd deal with that later.

'Later, Ralph,' Caleb said as they zoomed past.

Ralph lifted his head, stared at their joined hands and frowned. 'Caleb,' Ralph said, nodding slightly. 'Ava. Will we see you tonight?'

Her hand clenched in his and Caleb clenched back. And just like that she relaxed.

'Of course, Dad. Maybe we can get you to play a tune or two on Damien's harmonica.'

Caleb heard the catch in her voice and he pulled her a tad closer. She sank against him as though she needed the support in that moment. And he let her. No matter how good it felt and how much he'd regret allowing her vulnerability to get to him by the time the two of them were away from this place and alone together.

Ralph nodded again and the frown cleared up. 'Perhaps,' he said, then went back to his paper.

Caleb then pulled her down the stairs until he felt her pulling back.

'What's the hurry?' she asked.

'No hurry.'

'Good, because I don't have my purse, or keys to the house or anything.'

'You won't need them where we're going. Besides, you

still have that book clutched tight in your hand—what else have you ever needed?'

She grinned. 'Fair point. So where are we going exactly?'

'You'll see.'

In fact he thought he'd better come up with somewhere fast or else they'd be driving around in circles with that warm body and warm scent sending him further and further around the bend.

They reached the front of the house, complete with its two-storey columns, twin chimneys and wide sprawling white brick and charcoal shingle facing it looked like something the Kennedys would feel right at home in.

'Tell me that's not your car,' Ava said, tugging against his hand as they neared the low-slung, curvaceous, canary-yellow sports number parked at an askew angle on the white gravel drive.

'Ava, meet my favourite blonde. This is Mae West,' he said as he opened the door and swept an arm towards the cream leather passenger seat.

Her expression was mightily unimpressed, with him or the car. He only laughed. There weren't that many women in the world who'd not swoon over such ridiculously expensive an example of motor engineering while they dreamed of diamonds and cruises and fabric samples for the summer house.

But not Ava. She tucked herself into the seat as though she was trying to touch as little of the surrounding luxury as possible.

'You're a snob, you know that?' he said.

'Hey—'

He shut the door on her wounded expression.

He didn't have time to argue. He'd just spent the past four hours indulging in the longest concentrated foreplay of his young life. He needed her away from this place. It messed with her head and he wanted her thinking to be crystal-clear.

He opened the driver's side door, slid into spot and before she'd even got a word out said, 'Put on your seat belt.'

'I was. I am.'

'Good. It's just that with the way you've been all over me today I don't trust you not to get a sudden desire to jump me while we're driving.'

He turned the key, revved the noisy engine and he shot down the driveway and out onto Stonnington Drive. And anything she might have said in response was lost within the sound of the engine.

Hundred-year-old oak trees on either side of the road shaded the wide old street, lending the already elegant large houses a peaceful, austere quality. Though very few of the people living behind the façades were peaceful or austere. Most of them were stark raving mad.

But Caleb wouldn't begrudge a one of them a dime. They'd all made his childhood an interesting one to say the very least.

Ava made a small sigh beside him. He glanced sideways to find her looking out the window. Twelve-foot fences, ostentatious security gates and overly manicured brush-box hedges flickered over her reflection. But they couldn't hide her frown.

He slid into a higher gear and picked up speed. He felt as if he was losing ground. While her mere proximity still had him thrumming from head to toe.

There was no way that would all come to nothing. He had every intention of finishing what they'd started the day before. Especially after the way she had trembled at his every touch, and her skin had pinked every time they'd made eye contact.

His car growled at him as he took the corner a tad too fast.

Once they were off Stonnington Drive she seemed to come to as if from a trance. Her shoulders relaxed against the back of the seat and her head lolled sideways to face him.

That face. Who knew that after all these years that face could still drive him crazy? The speed limit soon became more of a guide than a rule.

'I'm not a snob,' she said.

And he laughed, enjoying feeling crazy a heck of a lot. 'Welcome back.'

Her mouth twisted. 'Sorry. Did I zone out mid-conversation?'

'Something like that.'

'Bad habit.'

Caleb took another sharp left, poor Mae West moaned from his rough handling. But now he knew where he was going he wanted to get there fast.

'Any chance you're going to fill me in on where you're taking me?' Ava asked when they swerved down a long driveway lined by massive pine trees.

'Weren't you the one who told me people don't like being asked too many obnoxious questions?' he said.

She couldn't hide her smile. 'That sure doesn't sound like me. Though if you answer my question there will be no more need for questions.'

He slowed the car to a crawl, the deep rumble of the engine rocking them from beneath. 'I can turn around and take you back home to the Halliburton Horror Mansion, or you can decide that where you really want to be more than anywhere else right now is where I have every intention of taking you.'

She stared at him for several long moments without blinking. The car began to feel hot as he waited for her response.

'Fine,' she said, the word shooting from her lips as though it had to fight its way through every last bit of common sense.

But Caleb wasn't looking for common sense. He was looking for submission. Now he had it. He pushed the accelerator to the floor.

Caleb slid his car into the private garage at the Stonnington Golf Links he spent a yearly fortune on so that his precious Mae was safe from little presents from the sky whenever he played there.

'You have to be kidding me,' Ava said when sensor lights flickered on as they drove in, showing off the wood-panelled walls and carpeted floor.

She spun on her seat, peering through the small back window as the garage door closed slowly behind them.

Caleb cut the engine.

Without the guttural roar the world around them suddenly fell quiet.

Ava turned back to face him, her eyes wide, dark, her breaths coming harder as she realised that they were well and truly alone for the first time since he'd left her the night before.

And that he'd planned it that way.

Her throat worked as she swallowed hard. But she didn't look away.

'Hi,' he said.

Her answering smile was fragile. 'Hi.'

He reached out and tucked a wave behind her ear. He left his hand around her neck, his thumb tracing the side of her throat.

'I was thinking we could go see if that spot by the fifth hole you used to like so much was still there.'

'How do you know about my spot by the fifth hole?'

'Every time I played as a kid you'd be there. Pretending to read.'

She nodded, then realised what he'd intimated. 'Hey!'

He slid his hand around the back of her neck and she melted against his touch. He hadn't imagined her response to him the night before. Thank the Lord.

'It was a very good spot for reading and reading only,' she said.

He'd always thought it a good spot for spying on him, but the last thing he wanted was to break the glorious sexual tension weaving its way around them by suggesting such a thing.

Ridiculous as it would seem at any other time, right then he desperately wished he owned a family sedan. One with nice big front seats that bent back all the way. Mae West's rather cramped interior was not conducive to what was about to happen.

He slid his hand away, only able to as he knew he'd be touching her again soon. He alighted from the car and went around to her side to open her door for her. She held out a hand, he took it and lifted her out.

They stood chest to chest.

He could feel the thunderous beat of her heart. It more than matched his own.

He'd held off long enough. He practically felt like some kind of saint for lasting as long as he had.

'Oh, to hell with it,' he said, wrapping a hand behind her neck and dragging her into his arms and kissing her.

Fireworks exploded behind Ava's eyes as she closed them tight and kissed Caleb right on back. Hard, fast, no holds barred.

Until that moment she had no idea how much she'd been craving this. Craving him. His touch, his taste. How little the night before had done to assuage the tension brimming between them.

That had been about a purely selfish, desperate need to clear her head, by using a man she knew could do just that.

As he pressed her back against the car, the hot metal no match for the heat sluicing between them, she didn't want to analyse what *this* was all about. She just wanted to live it. No motives, no consequences, just feelings and experience and pleasure.

She shut down the voices in her head and wrapped her arms around him, pressing herself along his length and sinking into his kiss as if it were the only way she could hope to ever breathe fully again.

He let her go to rid himself of his jacket, but their lips didn't part. The kiss was too good to forfeit. She unzipped her own tracksuit top and ripped it off her arms, letting it land in a heap at her feet. Hell, the floor in this garage was likely cleaner than the one in her dorm.

Then his hands were beneath her T-shirt, sliding over her skin. So warm. No, so *hot*. Knowing just where and how to touch her to make her melt. She shuddered deliciously.

All too soon, feeling as if she was about to pass out from the intensity of it all, she pulled away. Lay a hand on his chest. Took several deep breaths.

Caleb merely took it as an opportunity to rid her of her T-shirt, sliding it up her torso and over her head.

Memories of their first time came swarming back to her, but were soon crowded out by the current of sensation sweeping over her in the here and now.

Caleb's teeth at her neck, his hands cupping her bottom, his big, masculine body hard against her.

This had none of the innocence, none of the gentle finesse of anything they'd experienced together before. They were both grown-ups now. Both more well versed in desire. And both more desperate to simply have one another to bother with romance.

'You smell better than anyone I've ever known,' she said, sinking her face into his neck.

He brushed her hair aside and smiled against her cheek. 'I bet I do.'

She turned her head to give him better access. 'Though that could be because my sense of smell has been permanently damaged from too many years spent living in student accommodation.'

He moved to her ear lobe, sucking it into his mouth, before blowing soft, hot air across it. She arched against him.

'That'll teach you to sass me, Doc,' he said.

She slowly wrapped her leg around his calf and ran her hands through the back of his hair. God, she'd always loved his hair. The adorable curl, the preppy colour. It was beautifully coarse beneath her fingers.

He looked deep into her eyes.

'Is that all it took to get you to finally up your game? Sass,' she said, her voice as husky as all get out. 'Noted.'

His smile became a grin. A knowing, devilish grin that made her stomach clench in a mix of jitters and intense anticipation.

He slowed, brushed her hair from both shoulders. Slid a bra strap down one arm. Released her left breast to the open air. Cupped it with his hand. All the while watching her eyes cloud with the bliss of it all.

'You done sassing me?' he asked.

She nodded. Yes, yes, yes! Whatever it would take for him to stop the sweet torture.

As though she'd said the words aloud he ran his hand down her chest, circling her nipple, stroking her sensitive waist, pressing into her hip bone, and tugging open the top button of her jeans.

The sound of her zip split the air, his fingers slid beneath her panties and before she even had the chance to prepare herself for his touch he was working his magic.

She clung to him, her fingers curling into his sweater as the world around her slipped away and she felt every single sensation bombarding her.

Caleb's slow steady breaths tickled her hair. The robust curve of him clenched beneath the knee she had curled about his leg. And he stroked her until every feeling inside her, every sensation outside her collided into a small hot ball of pleasure that only built and built and built to such a crescendo she thought she might implode.

Just as she made to cry out Caleb kissed the sound away, taking her breath, her thoughts, her words, her release into him.

As she came down she realised the fingers clinging to his sweater hurt from hanging on so tight. She uncurled them just enough to let the blood back into her hands.

Then gathered her strength and looked up into his eyes. They were dark as night yet brilliant with desire. She could feel how great his strain from holding back.

She felt utterly powerful and terribly weak all at once.

She slowly pulled him towards her, and kissed him long and slow and deep.

And soon she was lost to his longing, his expertise, his burning heat all over again.

He lifted her so that her legs wrapped around him. Her eyes locked with his as he walked her to the front of the car. Then sat her upon the still-hot bonnet.

'Hot, hot!' she cried out.

'Tell me about it,' he murmured, and the car had nothing on the temperature of her skin.

'I meant the car,' she managed to breathe out. 'It's scorching.'

He frowned. Whipped his T-shirt and sweater over his head in that sexy back to front way men had of doing so. Silly the way that small move made Ava's already weak knees begin to quake.

He lay them on the hood, slid his hands beneath her backside, lifted her, then set her back upon his clothes.

'Better?'

She smiled, running hands over the tight hard muscles of his bare arms. 'My hero,' she purred.

His neck pinked. 'Don't go getting any ideas, Ava. I'm no gentleman.'

'Lucky me,' she said, before she dragged him down with her.

Caleb showed no mercy, touching, stroking, kissing, caressing every erogenous zone she had, plus a few she was sure only worked under his ministrations. And just as she began to peak all over again Caleb shucked off his shoes and jeans, tugged hers off with such dexterity and speed she found herself laughing from the craziness of it all.

When he fished a condom from his pocket, and fitted it, her laughter dried up in her throat. He poised his large form over her and looked into her eyes, letting her know that this was truly the point of no return.

As if she hadn't already leapt over that cliff.

He slid inside her, filling her so deeply her eyes closed and she held on for dear life as he took her places she hadn't even imagined she could go.

Never in her life had she felt as free. As liberated. As much all woman. To get there it had taken someone who was truly free, truly liberated, and all man.

And as together they moved and clung they fell apart in one another's arms.

The roar in Ava's head wafted away and slowly everything went quiet again. Her body took longer to come back to earth.

The room felt like a sauna. Her skin was drenched in sweat. Tendrils of her hair clung to her cheeks. She licked her lips to find they tasted of salt.

'Whoa,' Caleb finally said, his voice sounding as if he'd swallowed sandpaper.

'That's the word I've been looking for,' she said back.

He slowly lifted her upright, of which she was glad. Her equilibrium was not what it used to be. He slid his arms from around her, leaving her be, sitting atop the bonnet of the luxury car like some creature at an auto show. Funny, it was so outside her everyday existence it only made her feel even sexier.

'Pleased in the end that I brought you here?' he asked, standing before her butt naked and not in the least embarrassed about it, though why he should be she had no idea. All those tight, hard, youthful, male planes.

'Ecstatic,' she said, crossing her legs, her arms, anything she could to cover up as the cool fluorescent light flickering in the metal ceiling above did its best to illuminate everything in its path.

'Mmm,' he said, taking her hand and leading her off the car to where their clothes were scattered on the plush carpet. 'Next time you'll not argue and simply trust that I know best.'

'Next time?'

All she got for her sass that time was a slow, sexy smile.

And this time, rather than turning their backs and trying to forget what they'd done, they helped one another get dressed.

Caleb held out her jeans for her to step into. She bit her lip to stop from laughing as he nibbled at her hip bone.

Her eyes roved over his athletic chest as she took her time turning his inside-out T-shirt and sweater back the right way around for him.

And every time she slid her bra strap over her shoulder, he casually slid it back down again.

'Caleb,' she warned.

'Ava,' he said with a glint in his eye that made her completely satiated body begin to buzz with expectation again.

When she was again fully dressed he gave her one last tidy, straightening her top, zipping her jeans, wiping her damp hair back off her face with two sure hands. His eyes roved over her, making sure she looked put together, then he gave her a confident nod.

If the sex had been explosive, the aftermath was just about the most tender experience of her life.

At first she couldn't find the words to tell him so. And by the time she could she'd decided those intimacies were things best left unsaid.

It had been sex. Pure and simple. There was no mistake bigger than believing with Caleb it could ever mean more.

'So how about we head down to the fifth tee?' Caleb asked.

She flattened her palms over his sweater, ironing out the creases she'd put there. 'That's why you brought me here, right?'

He tucked her hand in his, pressed a button to open the garage door and said, 'Think that if you must.'

Ava blinked against the sunshine, hoping it would allow her a little time to bask in the aftermath before its bright restorative light brought everything back to real life.

CHAPTER NINE

FIFTEEN minutes later Caleb and Ava lay beneath a cloud of drooping willow leaves in a small thicket of trees on the edge of the fifth hole of the Stonnington Golf Links.

Caleb used his jacket as a cushion and her head rested on his thighs. Her sneakers and his rested in a haphazard pile at the base of a tree. And she felt as if the afterglow would last for ever.

She glanced sideways to find him leaning back on his forearms. A large round diving watch gleamed expensively at the end of a well-sculpted, tanned arm. His dark jeans wrapped around his thighs as though his muscles were straining to be free. A long piece of grass twirled between his teeth.

Her insides did that awful twisting thing they'd been doing all weekend. Ten years studying at the hardest schools in the world and her constitution had been fine. One weekend back on Stonnington Drive and she was developing an ulcer.

In front of them the perfect green rolled away from them towards a lake filled with waving rushes and brown wood ducks. While behind them and down a deep gully was a meandering creek which cut through her parents' backyard. 'You couldn't have taken me further away, by any chance?' she asked.

After a lazy pause he said, 'Now that's not what you came back to Melbourne for, was it?'

She grimaced. He was right.

He'd been spot on earlier too. She had been able to secretly, or not so secretly as it turned out, watch Caleb and his father during their weekly game from this vantage point. Even as a teenager he'd fitted in as though he'd been genetically engineered for the lifestyle they'd been born into.

With his boyish curls and his neat white teeth. His long, lanky, lackadaisical stride. His utter cool in the face of anything life threw at him. His ace tennis serve, his perfect golf swing, the packs of girls who'd followed him around like bees to pollen.

Yet the spark of brilliance he'd always carried with him had nothing to do with advantage or privilege. It was deeper than that. He had the exceptional kind of innate magnetism that meant a regular girl like her found herself naked atop a sports car.

Caleb breathed long and hard through his nose and the muscles of his chest pressed against the fabric of his T-shirt. The boy was all grown up. And didn't she now know just how?

A fly buzzed by her nose. She swatted it away, angry at it for spoiling the decadent idyll she was thoroughly enjoying. But it only came back.

Buzz buzz buzz. This can't last.

The last of her happy haze wore off as life rudely intruded. But it was for the best. She only had a couple of days before she was due back at school and if anything in her life was ever going to be different, if she was ever going to stop repeating the same mistakes over and over again, she had to begin with a clean slate. With her parents. With this place. With this man. And that didn't just mean exorcising lingering feelings she had for him.

She picked up a leaf from the ground and began peeling it apart. 'Do you remember the last time we played golf here?'

Caleb's eyes narrowed, but he kept his gaze on whatever he was staring at in the distance. 'You mean the only time. When you lost every one of the dozen balls you started out with. And the golf pro suggested perhaps you have lessons. Elsewhere.'

'Yeah, that time. I thought I was showing some potential.' She sat up, leant back on her hands so that she looked down into his untroubled face and chose her next words carefully. 'If I hadn't have left I may have become some kind of golfer.'

He rolled onto one elbow, pulled the grass from his mouth, flicked it away and looked into her eyes. 'Well, then, I guess you should never have left.'

She blinked down at him. The guy was just too cluey. She should have remembered that. She might well have duxed every school she'd ever attended, but Caleb had always managed to make her feel as if she was playing catch up.

'I had to leave,' she said, resolutely sticking to her train of thought. 'My life here wasn't healthy.'

'I can't imagine a healthier life to be had.'

'You think? I found out about the birds and the bees from Caroline Vance out the back of the Science lab in third grade. She'd given Jamie Crowson her lunch money to show us what he had down the front of his shorts.'

Caleb's laughter echoed so loudly in their little grove it created waves of pleasure over her skin.

'It's not funny!' she said. 'I close my eyes and I can still see his Spiderman underpants.'

Caleb's laughter only grew.

Ava sank her face into her open palms and tried to think of a happy place. But she realised that sitting beneath this tree, next to this guy, his laughter reverberating dizzily in the back of her head, was about the happiest she'd been in some time.

'I can't believe I felt I might now be able to share a torturous childhood moment with you.'

'What, now that I've had you naked against the bonnet of a Lamborghini suddenly you see me as your Dear Diary? How nice.'

'No,' she said, putting the backs of her hands against her hot cheeks. 'I meant now that you're supposedly all grown up. But you haven't changed.'

'You have.' He glanced her way before finding his naked toes suddenly fascinating. 'As to your predicament, true, your parents can be a pain in the proverbial, but you can't possibly tell me you didn't have everything to stay for.'

Everything to stay for...

The only thing she'd wanted to stay for had been him. Choosing between the slight possibility of him and the reality of Harvard had been ridiculously difficult. In the end her own indecisiveness had been the clincher.

'I did not want to become my mother,' she said.

His eyes narrowed. 'What on earth—?'

'Playing tennis three times a week but never finding time to do kinder duty at my kids' schools. Redecorating the kitchen every two years because I have nothing else to do. Drinking martinis at nine in the morning.'

'Bloody Marys.'

'Excuse me?'

'She's moved on to Bloody Marys. On a health kick, don't you know.'

She shook her head. 'I hate tomato juice so that only shows how much I would have regretted that life. You know I love her. I do. She's so stunningly oblivious one can't help but love my mother. But the last thing I ever want to become is her.'

'You couldn't become Rachel Halliburton if you dyed your hair blonde and wore a tennis skirt twenty-four-seven.'

'Who says? I love the house I grew up in. I loved hanging out with the kids on the block. With you.' She glanced his way to find he was staring out into the distance again. 'I loved my private education and having no government debt to worry about. It's a slippery slope.'

He shrugged as much as a man resting back on his elbows could shrug. She kind of wished he'd sit up and face her. She didn't see how anyone could have a serious conversation when they looked so relaxed. So cool. So provocative all stretched out like a lion basking in the sun.

She wondered if he ever really cared about anything the way she couldn't help but care so much about everything.

'Your father misses you terribly,' he said, catching her unawares.

She shook her head, vigorously, enough that she had to fix her hair afterwards. 'I'm pretty sure he has no clue I ever left. Probably looks up from his newspaper once a month and figures I've gone out for ice cream again.'

'He knows,' Caleb said. 'He adores you, Doc. Damien was always self-sufficient. I reckon the guy was born in a suit and tie. But you were always your father's little princess. Anyone seeing the two of you together could see it. Everyone including your stunningly oblivious mother, who no doubt wondered what she had to do to get the same level of attention.'

Ava had never seen it that way. Yet it somehow made all kinds of sense. She pulled her knees to her chest. 'Once upon a time maybe.'

'Uh, no. When he saw us coming down the stairs together last night for a moment I actually feared for my life.'

'Don't be ridiculous.'

'I'm serious. Your father has always been a bear of a man. The only times I've ever seen him smile with teeth is when he's beating someone at golf or if the stock reports in that day's financial section of the paper were in his favour. But when he saw you yesterday, his eyes, they melted. You reduced him to a puppy dog. And then when he saw I was with you, the kid he'd always kept a close eye on lest I lead his respectable son astray, and deduced where we had been...'

Ava held her hands over her eyes. 'No-o-o. My father did not deduce anything.'

'Then why did he look at me as though he was trying to remember where he'd last seen a meat cleaver? He's a large man, your father. Possibly the only man I've ever met who I'd not back myself against in a street brawl.'

Ava rested her chin on her upper arm and stared at him. 'And when have you ever pictured yourself in a street brawl?'

Caleb laughed some more, the deep, heavenly sound lulling her into wanting to stretch out sideways until she was lying beside him. Tucked in against his solid chest.

As though her need had reached out to him, he placed a hand around her bare foot. His simple touch made her feel hot and loose all over again, heaven help her.

'You, my sweet,' he said, 'obviously have no idea how men's minds work.'

'That,' she said, curling her toes into the grass, 'is an understatement.'

As Caleb softly massaged her foot the world beneath her began to tip and tumble. She reached down and let the dirt and twigs at her sides dig into her soft palms.

So much for exorcising him from her system.

They'd locked horns since the day they'd met and still didn't quite know how to disentangle them. Perhaps because neither of them truly wanted to. Oh, boy...

'Did you know that dendrophobia is the fear of trees?' she blurted.

Caleb blinked just the once, then he let go of her foot and let his gaze wander back to the fairway. 'Sure. Everybody knows that.'

Ava frowned. 'Really?'

'No. Nobody knows that. Why would anybody know that?'

'If they'd spent any time studying the basics of psychological phobias they might.'

'Right. Of course. In my spare time between women's studies and advanced keg emptying I must have missed that class at uni.'

Thankful for the chance to keep her own problems out of the limelight for the moment, she said, 'From what Damien has told me, you are some kind of star in the business world. Unmatched at what you do. You shouldn't demean what you've achieved.'

'Me? Why on earth would I do that? I'm a hell of a guy. Just ask me.'

'Yet before I left you seemed to be trying your very best to have as dissolute a university life as you could.'

'As opposed to…'

'As opposed to the extraordinary one I always thought you capable of. I wondered if that was the result of your being an only child. The expectations must have been exhausting.'

She blinked several times, waiting for his response to what she thought a well-reasoned proposition if she did say so herself.

He gradually pressed himself into a sitting position so that they saw eye to eye. So that she could feel his breath against her cheeks. That sexy smile of his tickled at the corners of his mouth before he said, 'You thought me extraordinary?'

'With the opportunities we had we had no right not to be extraordinary.'

His smile deepened. *Oh, boy, oh, boy, oh, boy…*

Then he reached up and ran a hand through her hair. Her breath hitched in her throat. Her every muscle froze. Until his fingers came away with a twig. He held it between them, then crushed it between his strong fingers.

He stared at the broken pieces as he said, 'So it wasn't just that you thought me *extra* special.'

She felt her cheeks pinking. Then as his eyes once again found hers she frantically searched the ground for another leaf to decimate, but it seemed she'd pretty much made a mess of every one within a metre radius of her position.

'Perhaps you're right,' he said.

'About what?' she croaked.

'I was doing my very best to negate the advantages I'd been given. The day I realised it everything changed. The good life and I have been firm friends ever since.'

He made fun. But she knew it was more than that. He was a success in every sense of the word. While she'd lived a life of perpetual adolescence sleeping in smelly dorms, or on friends' foldaway beds, dating father-figures in search of some kind of substitute approval she hadn't had from her own dad.

Yeah, she wasn't as clueless as people seemed to think she was. She'd learnt a thing or two about herself while studying psychology. But a person who knew themselves didn't necessarily make a person who knew how to fix themselves. Except, it seemed, for Caleb.

'I guess I can't have expected ten years to have gone by and nothing have changed,' she said.

'Though some things will never change no matter how many years you give them in the hopes they might.' The shadow of a sensitive smile darted across his face before it was quickly swallowed up by his usual intentionally indolent expression. And it made her heart thump in several wrong directions before it found its rhythm again.

She searched for some random snippet of trivia she could throw into the mix to snap the loaded tension. But his proximity muddled her brain. Made her ache for him. Made her lick her lips and imagine going for round two right here, right now under the noses of goodness knew how many Sunday golfers.

She had no excuse, no beer, no music, no romance of a wedding, or rumble of a fast car to use as an excuse for the feelings devastating her.

Just the scent of fresh grass clippings, the soft song of birds in the trees above, and Caleb filling her vision. Big, bad, beautiful Caleb.

As though he knew exactly what she was thinking he leaned across her, resting his hand on the other side of her leg so that she was trapped. 'So tell me,' he drawled, 'did you ever meet any guys like me over across the sea and far away?'

'Thankfully there is no one else in the world quite like you. You?'

'Hmm?'

'Ever find yourself with anyone quite like me?'

'What—opinionated, in need of a hairbrush, two left feet?'

Time swirled about her, sliding back into the past for a brief moment before it settled right back to the present. She hadn't seen the man in nigh on ten years and he'd summed her up in a sentence. No one anywhere in the world knew her quite so well.

And then just before she quite came back to earth he kissed her. Yielding, slow, timeless kisses that made her bones dissolve.

His stubble tickled her cheeks. His teeth nipped at her bottom lip. The thumb of his right hand trailed up and down her bare ankle.

Feelings and sensations tumbled inside her. She grabbed a handful of his T-shirt in an attempt to stay steady. But it was no use.

Everything in her life was already so far out of control and this was the only kind of out of control she could take more of.

The kiss ended. Her hand uncurled from the front of his shirt. And her heart felt as if it were sitting outside her chest. Bare. Naked. Exposed.

'That night, in the boat shed, before I left,' she said, the words bubbling up from goodness knew where, 'you were my first.'

He reached up and ran a hand through her hair, and this time he twirled a wave around his finger before letting it fall back to her shoulder. 'I know,' he said.

She cringed. 'Was it that obvious?'

He nodded just the once. 'In the best way.'

'Now you're just being nice. I'm not sure I can handle you nice.'

'Why? What do you think you might do?'

'Heavens. Nothing worse than what we've already done.'

'We haven't done anything wrong. Or bad. In fact I think it's all been pretty good.'

She licked her bottom lip and his eyes grew darker.

'Maybe that's why it feels so good,' she said. 'Because we both really know it's bad.'

'I like bad.'

'No surprise there. I had no idea that *I* liked bad. But now I'm kind of getting the hang of it.'

His face eased into the kind of smile that would have crumpled the knees from beneath her had she not already been sitting. 'I can attest to that.'

'Why, thank you.'

'No,' he said. 'Thank you.'

Ava let her gaze rove over every inch of his face. She'd need something good to take back with her to school where she was about to face more than just the review committee, but possibly the ridicule and collapse of her academic future.

It was a beautiful face. Charming, sinfully arresting, full of character. Those hot hazel eyes of his made her heart race.

And he knew it. She could see it in those same eyes. She tipped her head forward, hiding behind a curtain of hair. 'I didn't come to you that day in the boat shed looking for what I found.'

'I never for a moment thought you had.'

She shook her hair from her face and looked him dead in the eye.

She waited for him to say more. To say it had been special, important, or even the slightest bit meaningful. In the end, his silence spoke volumes. They might well have been naked in one another's arms an hour earlier, but she was the only one with her heart on her sleeve.

As such, confession time was over.

She managed to get herself to her feet without touching him. With that kind of dexterity she could have been a gymnast in another life.

She grabbed her shoes and brushed herself off. 'Come on, Caleb. Even though I'm sure nobody even remembers we're gone, we'd better get back. This weekend is all about the bride and groom, after all.'

He lifted a hand to her and she had no choice but to grab on with both of hers and pull. He pushed his heavy self to his feet and looked down at her, dark eyes further shadowed by the waterfall of willow leaves concealing them from the world at large.

'So do you feel better now?' he asked.

'Excuse me?'

'Now that you've ticked me off your list?'

'What list?'

'The I'm-going-to-make-up-for-past-mistakes list.'

She looked down. 'That's not what I'm doing.'

He held a finger beneath her chin and lifted it until she had no choice but to look in his eyes. 'You don't need everybody in the world to like you, you know. Hell, even some of my closest acquaintances can't stand me half the time.'

'I don't need everybody to like me,' she said. *Just the ones who should love me.*

His finger left her chin and ran down the side of her cheek, tucking her hair behind her ear. 'Maybe you haven't changed that much after all.'

He leaned in, kissed her softly on the mouth, then turned her and gave her a little shove out of their secluded glade and into the overbright sunshine.

Easy for him to say, she thought as she stamped down the path back to the car. *Everything has always come so easily to him.*

She'd been too studious to be popular at school. Able to chug back beers with too much ease to fit in with Taylor's wine and cheese friends. And after the divorce she'd always been too needy of garnering her father's attention to get it.

She'd never been able to find a place where she really fitted. No matter how far and wide she'd searched.

Then again sitting beside him on the couch sharing private jokes had been something she could have spent the whole day doing. And lying in her favourite glade with her head on Caleb's lap had felt like a little piece of heaven. But could any of that compare with how right it had felt to have her body intertwined with his?

It seemed the only place in the world she really fitted was with him. Rather than depressing her, for all its inconvenience it set off a light bulb inside her head.

Perhaps this weekend she ought to give the guy everything until she had nothing left to give. Then with a perfectly clean slate maybe she'd finally be able to form a healthy relationship with someone more suitable. More available. More local. And less likely to turn her head so far she'd end up facing the wrong way.

She'd just have to make sure that this time, unlike last time, she'd be okay. She was older. Stronger. This time she was forewarned.

For the last time she'd loved him and left him she'd spent the whole plane ride to London in tears. So much so the stewardess had taken her into a spare seat in first class to calm her down and let the others in economy get some sleep.

CHAPTER TEN

LATER that evening, after everyone had played their part in the procession of luxury cars ferrying the trillion-odd wedding gifts to Damien and Chelsea's new nearby house, the Halliburton family circus returned home for a family-only barbecue.

Ava sat on a white cane chair on the terrace, her finger unconsciously running back and forth beneath the leather strap at her neck. She wished she'd thought to bring a book downstairs. A book had always given her a wall of privacy even when the Halliburton world raged around her.

Instead she was forced to watch on, from the outside looking in, as Damien manned the barbecue, Chelsea chased the naughty puppy off into the garden, her mother was in the kitchen likely giving the cook what for and Ralph stood by the barbecue, one hand in the pocket of his chinos, the other holding a beer, laughing.

Caleb was right. A lot had changed in the years since she'd been gone. She didn't remember her father ever drinking anything as pedestrian as a beer. Though it was imported…

He'd also said that some things never changed no matter how many years you gave them in the hopes they might. The guy was too laid-back to ever waste a breath, much less a dozen words. So just what had he meant by that?

Ava flinched at the sudden squeak of sneaker on tessellated tile.

Her mother appeared from outside the blur of her tunnel vision. 'Where's Caleb?'

She sank down deeper into the chair. 'How should I know?'

Her mother gave her one raised eyebrow. Ava felt her neck warming. Had she been the last one to figure that she and Caleb had unfinished business?

Ava said, 'He's not family, so I assume that's why he didn't show up to this family-only do.'

Her mother, long since immune to sarcasm, gave a small shrug, then bounced over to the barbecue.

Ava watched on as her mother touched her father on the shoulder as she leaned in to ask him something. He leant his cheek against the back of her hand a moment. Then he turned and kissed her knuckles, then walked back into the house.

It was a simple move. Yet achingly intimate. Ava might not have even noticed if she hadn't been paying such close attention.

It wasn't just about reciprocal needs met. Or the comfort and ease that came from knowing someone half your life. But care. Tenderness. Love.

'You see that?'

She blinked as Damien's voice cut into her reverie. He was standing over her shoulder, a plate of juicy cooked steaks on a platter in his arms.

She nodded slowly. 'They really are back together, aren't they?'

'I told you you'd need to see it to believe it.'

'You can't blame me after having a front-row seat as it all fell apart the first time.'

Damien squeezed her shoulder. 'Since he retired he and

Mum began catching up for coffee every now and then. Then they joined forces on the local seniors' tennis circuit. Mum still officially has her apartment but she's always here. I think they really don't know that the world knows they're back together. It's like a romantic little secret. And I'm happy for them to keep it that way if it makes them happy.'

Ava's eye twitched. And she bit at her bottom lip. For them to remain happy she couldn't say a word about it. But for her to find any kind of closure on that part of her life she knew she had to talk about it.

Her legs began to jiggle with all of the energy she was having to hold back.

She turned to her brother and tucked her feet beneath her on the chair. 'And you? You're deliriously happy, I take it.'

'Thanks to Chelsea, you bet I am,' her brother said, but his smile was all the answer she needed. 'Hey, where were you this arvo? Chelsea and I were hoping to have some time together, just the three of us. I feel like I've barely had any time with you this weekend.'

'Understandable, brother,' she said, chucking him on the arm. 'You have other things on your mind.'

His eyes narrowed. 'Where were you?' he repeated.

Ava swore beneath her breath that her little smoke-and-mirrors act hadn't worked. 'I was…umm—'

'With Caleb,' he finished for her.

She clicked her fingers. 'Right. With Caleb. Haven't seen him in years, you know. We just, you know, chatted about stuff we've done in the last ten years. Had a giggle about old times. My golf game. Stuff like that.'

Several taut seconds passed before Damien said, 'Well, so long as he's behaving himself. I made him promise to play nice.'

That had her sitting upright. 'You did what?'

He instantly backed out of hitting distance. 'The two of

you were always at one another as kids, and I wanted to make sure your trip home was as uneventful as possible without him making things more complicated.'

Complicated? The poor guy had no idea how complicated things had become and how much his words had just complicated things all the more.

'Caleb is not that complicated,' she said with as uncomplicated a smile as she could manage while she framed all sorts of words she'd have with Caleb when she next saw him.

Damien smiled back, but she wasn't sure she truly had him fooled. 'No. I guess he's not.'

And when his bride came bounding up the back steps with their new puppy in tow he gave Ava a kiss atop her head, then strode towards Chelsea as fast as his two feet could carry him.

Damien brushed stray waves from Chelsea's face and kissed her, and all Ava's energy simmered to a low boil.

She belonged in this scene less now than she ever had. Only now it was because everyone there was perfectly happy without her.

It was suddenly too much for Ava to bear. She felt as if she should never have come home at all.

She hopped off the lounger and went inside looking for space. And what she found was her father paused in the doorway, newspaper folded under one arm, a fresh beer in the other hand, a startled look in his eyes as though he was hoping he hadn't been seen.

'Dad,' she said on an expulsion of breath.

'Ava,' he said with a sharp nod.

That was all she was going to get? Again? She was quite simply too ruffled to let it slide this time. She stared at him as if to say, *And whatcha gonna do about it?*

He looked up and down the long terrace as though hoping to

find a private little area in which he could hole himself up. Alone.

She threw her arms out in defeat. 'Don't panic. I was just leaving.'

'No. There's no reason—'

'Like hell there isn't. If I had a mainsail and a keel I'd get more of a look in than I ever did in this family. I should never have come back here. Hoping it might be different. I might be different. You…'

He *was* different. The way he'd taken her mother back proved that. She was the one who still felt as if she were bobbing in unfamiliar seas.

'Oh, forget it.'

She knew it wasn't really him she was angry with any more. It was her. Or Caleb for not opening up to her as she had to him. But her dad was unfortunate enough to be in the line of fire, and she'd been angry at him at one time and never let him know about it. It seemed she was making up for a lot this weekend.

'I'll see you later,' she said as she angled past.

But before she even made it two steps he said, 'I'm no fool, child.'

She slowed up and her gaze shot to his. She looked from one dark blue eye to the other, hoping to find a flicker of consideration, or compassion. But all she saw was the man she'd grown up thinking hung the moon and the stars, the one who'd given her her first book, who'd never told her how to spell a word of her homework if she didn't first look it up in the dictionary, but who'd turned out to have feet of clay after all.

She took a deep breath to stop from turning into the heartbroken fourteen-year-old she always felt like around him. 'Dad, I never said you were a fool.'

'But you thought it,' her father said. 'I see it in your eyes, even now. You thought I was wrong to ask your mother to leave and you think I'm wrong now to have taken her back. And you've never forgiven me for either decision.'

Ava stared at him. Speechless.

He blinked twice before saying, 'I still remember the day you were born like it was yesterday.'

She gulped down a mouthful of dry air, which did nothing to soothe her suddenly aching throat.

'Your eyes always followed the sound of my voice. Your first smile was mine. The first time you reached out and gripped anything it was my little finger. When Damien was born I could have exploded with pride. But you were precious. My little girl. And now I look at you standing there, the same age I was when your mother and I had you, and I can't imagine where the years since have gone.'

His eyes were so sad it hurt her heart.

She squared her shoulders to open her chest so that she could breathe. 'I don't remember you picking up the phone to call me either, you know.'

He slapped the newspaper down onto the table, and when he looked back at her she might as well have slapped him fair across the cheek for the shock and anger she saw in him. And any kind of headway they might have made by her simply turning up came to a screeching halt.

'Dad—'

He held up his now free hand. 'You should never have gone to that blasted school. I should have made you stay. I shouldn't have counted on Caleb to do the asking. It should have been me.'

If she'd needed anything to help find her voice again that was it.

'Oh, you've got to be kidding me!' she cried. 'Did the guy

pay a town crier to go up and down Stonnington Drive that day?'

A muscle twitched in her father's jaw. 'At least he talks to this family about such things.'

It was too late by then. She was good and riled and nothing was going to stop her. 'And do you wonder why I don't?'

Her father dropped his chin and shook his head. It was several moments before he looked up again and if he'd been any other man she might have thought that glint in his eye was a tear. 'I don't wonder. I understand. And I lament the fact every day.'

A small breathless 'Oh,' escaped her lips. But before she had the chance to even come to terms with what that might mean, her father said:

'I lament that I was too caught up in the grand failure of my marriage to see that you were floundering on the sideline. And I lament that by the time I realised it, that the influence that boy had always had over you wasn't enough to get you through. He may have been as corrupting as all get out, but he has a good heart, a good head, good sense, and he always preferred you.'

Her galloping heart took a little stumble.

Caleb... Preferred her? Always?

She swallowed hard and lifted her chin. 'I shouldn't be surprised you wanted Caleb to do your dirty work. Nobody in this family bar Damien ever managed to string two words together in my direction from the moment Mum first walked out of here.'

Her father shook his head. 'I never thought I'd see the day when that little girl who once looked upon me with such adoration could become so flinty. And so unforgiving.'

She felt as if a hot knife had sliced through her heart.

Why she'd thought coming home would help her find her

path again, goodness only knew. At least from a distance she felt a little sad about the relationship she had with her parents.

And now... Now her father was looking at her with pure and unadulterated disappointment. She'd never in her life felt worse.

She turned her back on him and walked. Just walked. Through the kitchen, across the terrace, down the wide marble steps, across the back lawn and towards the bank of pristine conifers lining the edge of the property.

Pushing through the scratchy lower branches, she came upon the small cliff face that led to the river. The old mouldy steps Damien and Caleb had carved into the cliff face so that they could sneak out of the house as teenage boys were still there. Surely. Geography was one thing that couldn't change that much in ten years.

Unable to see them, she began to panic. She slid to her knees and scrambled about in the brush for the white stone marker, not caring that the knees of her jeans were soon covered in grass stains or her hands in mud.

She heaved a huge sigh of relief when she found the top step, then, placing one fast foot after the other, she half walked, half slid down the bank, hit the dank mossy edge of the stream cutting the house off from the golf course, stepped across the flat stones, her feet squelching in mud and low trickling water, until she was near the other side.

And that was where her life really hit its straps.

Not only was she not as practised or as nimble as she'd been at nineteen, her feet were a half-size bigger. She hit the last stone, her toes curled over the edge and her heel dangled off the back. There she teetered for a good five seconds, swaying back and forth, her arms held out like a tightrope walker.

And then with as much grace as a hippo trying ballet for the first time she landed butt first in the inch-high water.

Everything changed. Yet nothing ever changed.

Hang social anthropology and family politics, she thought. *Philosophy might be my calling after all.*

CHAPTER ELEVEN

CALEB wiped the shower fog from his bathroom mirror, and slapped cologne on his neck. He was preparing himself for what he hoped would be a big night out, a night of wine, women and song. Whatever it took to lose the constant slideshow of images of Ava Halliburton from the front of his mind.

Sure, they were nice images, but for some reason they were beginning to make him feel edgy. Wobbly around the edges. It wasn't a feeling he cared to name, or encourage.

There was a knock on his apartment door.

He poked his head out of the bathroom and glanced at the wagon-wheel clock over the bar. It was a little after seven in the evening.

He rubbed his towel over his still-wet hair, then wrapped it loosely around his hips and padded through the sunken lounge and up the three wide steps to the front door, leaving faint footprints on the hardwood floor.

He opened the door expecting it to be Pedro, his neighbour across the hall who was always in need of rubber bands, or self-raising flour, or a vase, or some such oddment.

But it wasn't Pedro. It wasn't even close to being Pedro.

It was Ava. The bottoms of her jeans were caked in mud. There were grass stains on her knees. And a small scratch on her chin, which looked as if it had been bleeding. But it was her bright eyes, shiny and wide as though she'd been crying, that made his heart twist in his chest.

'Barbecue over so soon?' he asked.

She burst past him, not even registering his state of undress. Something must have been really wrong.

'Something I can help you with?' he asked, rehitching his towel.

'It's my dad.'

'What a shocker,' Caleb said beneath his breath as he leant his backside against a hall table on the far side of the room.

'We just had an altercation at home. I knew I should never have stayed there. I should have stayed at the hotel as planned. Made this a civilised visit. In and out. But no-o-o. The minute my dad asks me to stay and I'm putty. Weak-willed little girl just wanting to please him. And you!' she said as she turned on him.

'And this has what to do with me—?'

'You told my father I was leaving.'

'I assumed you had a return ticket.'

'Not now. Then. When I went to Harvard. After that night…' She waved a fast hand over her face as though wiping out what she'd been about to say.

'I never said I hadn't told him.'

Her big blue eyes snapped to focus on his face then, her chin as stubborn as he'd ever seen it. 'What gave you the right?'

'Oh, I don't know. The fact that I knew that your parents would be beside themselves if they woke up one morning and you were gone.'

'That was my choice. Waiting until I got there to tell them had been my decision. I was terrified to call them when I arrived in London and they already knew!'

She took up her pacing with such frenzy she was leaving track marks in the plush cream rug by his fireplace. 'I'm twenty-nine, for goodness' sake. These things shouldn't affect me the way they do.'

'When you're fifty-nine you'll still be your father's daughter whether you like it or not.'

She glanced at him as though seeing him for the first time. And even though he was doing his very best to remain unaffected by her, his skin was of a different mind—heating, itching—as he imagined her in nothing but a towel, and then less as she wrapped herself around him.

'This is some place you've got here,' she said, turning from him and jogging up the steps to the wall-to-wall windows overlooking the Melbourne city skyline. 'Wow, that view is gorgeous.'

It was just the kind of view that put a woman in a romantic mood. All multicoloured city lights sparkling off the Yarra. And the great Flinders Street train station reposing like a great sphinx on the far bank.

Yet for some reason Caleb was careful to keep a piece of furniture between him and Ava at all times.

His phone rang. Ava spun and stared at it as though it might be about to explode. Caleb let it go to his machine.

From the phone her eyes moved to rove over his loft-style apartment. Over the plush leather sofas in the sunken lounge. Over the polished wood floors, the state-of-the-art raised kitchen and up the winding staircase to his second-floor bedroom.

It changed her focus. Calmed her. The manic whirlwind settled. Her movements became more relaxed. The great accommodating whoosh of air that had clouded his head the moment she'd exploded into his home subsided.

And he couldn't take his eyes off her.

At some stage she'd changed into dark denim jeans and a pink T-shirt with a picture of Little Miss Sunshine on it. It was fitted, and short enough that every time she moved it revealed a sliver of creamy skin above the beltline of her jeans.

Her hair was up in a shaggy mess atop her head. Her foul mood had only served to put apples in her cheeks. And her lips were hot pink from her biting at them continuously since she'd come in.

He clenched his teeth and dug his fingers hard into the knot of his towel to stop himself from moving an inch in her direction.

Once her tirade was over she'd go. He'd make her. He'd turn her around and send her on her way and he could go back to getting ready to go out. Away from here. Away from her.

Her gaze slunk down the stairs and back to him. It seemed to linger on his towel for a few moments. Her chest expanded as she took in a deep long breath. Then she looked him dead in the eye.

Her eyes narrowed. 'Do your parents own this place?'

If he'd needed something to quench his urge to push aside every piece of furniture to get to her that did it.

'No, Ava, I am a grown man with a big-boy job for which I earn dollars to pay for such nice things.'

'That's right, you work for Damien.'

'We're partners at Keppler, Jones and Morgenstern. Fifty-fifty profit share split down the middle.' *Thank you very much.*

She frowned some more.

'I'm not sorry that I come from privilege, Ava. I feel privileged to have come from privilege. I like that I don't have to worry about where my next Lamborghini will come from. Sorry if that messes with your socialist outlook. I only hope it's kept you warm at night as much as my five-hundred-dollar sheets and goose-down comforter have me.'

'You have a point. Who needs autonomy when one has central heating?' She turned away from the window and ambled back down the stairs towards him and that was when he saw the glint in her eye.

She hadn't come here because she was in a snip at all. She knew just what she was doing and right now that entailed teasing him.

A primal growl rumbled to life in his throat. Oh, he ached to make her pay. For leaving all too easily all those years ago. For making him so crazy now. He did not need this. Didn't need her. But damn it if he didn't want her still.

It was then that he realised there was now no longer anything between them but wide-open space and a black Egyptian cotton towel.

'How did you get here, Ava?' he asked, his voice tight.

'Taxi.'

'Not the proletariat train for you?'

She pointed a finger at his chest. 'I thought Damien told you to be nice to me.' Her mouth twisted for a second before she smiled. 'His wallet was on the kitchen bench. So I nicked twenty bucks.'

Caleb laughed.

Ava snuck closer. 'I was upset. With Dad for putting me in my place. And Mum for always getting what she wants. And Damien and Chelsea for being so happy. It seems being bad is for me after all.'

She was beside him now. She picked up a piece of unopened mail, turned it over in her hand to read the sender's address, then put it back on the glass bowl on the hall table.

'So your dad put you in your place, did he?'

She nodded. 'He called me flinty and unforgiving.'

Caleb winced.

She shrugged. 'I know. Harsh. But no less than I deserved. The cab ride over here was long enough for me to admit that you were right about one thing.'

'Just the one?' He looked at her mouth. He couldn't help himself. It was just so pink, and soft, and he could still feel its imprint on his.

'I think he's sorry. I think he wishes we'd had a better relationship. I think, I think, I think, but I won't know unless I do forgive him and stop being such a sorry excuse for a daughter and blah blah blah.' She shook out her hands. 'Okay. Enough for today.'

She glanced at his towel again and this time licked her lips. 'Did I interrupt you doing something?'

'Me?' Caleb put a hand to his naked chest.

Ava's eyes followed. Darkened.

He cleared his throat. 'I was getting ready to go out.'

She looked up. Frowned. 'Oh. I was kidding. I'm sorry, I just, I needed to clear my head and somehow every time I spend time with you I seem to think more clearly for some reason, so I thought… I guess I should leave you to get ready.'

'Fine.'

She didn't move an inch.

'Do you need money for a cab?' he asked.

She shook her head, and her shoulders and her hips. Swinging left to right and back again until he felt as if he were fast becoming hypnotised.

'Right, then.'

He moved to the front door. Opened it. She slunk past and out into the hall. The scent of orange blossoms filled his nose. He gripped the door handle until his knuckles turned white.

'You're a good guy, Caleb Gilchrist.'

'Don't you go thinking that now, Ava Halliburton. I've known smarter women than you get into a whole load of trouble thinking such rubbish.'

Her brow furrowed. 'You've known smarter women than me?'

He laughed. A belly laugh that rumbled all the way to the ends of his naked limbs and back again.

He reached out and ran his thumb down her chin. 'Never have. Never will.'

She glanced down the hallway, biting at her lip. Her brow furrowed as though she hadn't thought past this part. 'Well,' she said, 'I guess I'd better head back.'

'Perhaps you should.'

He could have closed the door in her face. Hell, he could have taken a solo chair that morning for the present-opening ceremony. He could have said hello the night before then spent the rest of the evening chatting up a wedding guest.

But Ava Halliburton was his Achilles' heel. Always had been and by the looks of things she always would be. From the second he'd seen her sitting in the church he'd been toast.

The only answer was to reduce her the same way. To teach her that playing with fire would only get her burnt.

He reached out, slid a hand sensuously down her arm. For the first time since she'd landed in his apartment she seemed unsure.

'How about a proper goodbye?' he said, his voice gruff.

Slowly. Achingly slowly he drew her back inside. And when she was close enough he could see her eyes were dark pools of anticipation.

'Goodbye, Ava,' he said, smiling as he leaned in to kiss her.

The kiss was slow, sensual and searching. As ever before she melted into him with such effortlessness, such trust. She made it so easy for her pleasure to become his pleasure and that was enough.

Her cool hands slunk around his waist. The texture of cotton and flesh sliding against his naked torso and his warm skin contracted delectably beneath her touch. He reached up and pulled the comb from her hair. Her waves tumbled heavily into his hands until they became blissfully knotted.

And they kissed and kissed and kissed.

Their lips parted as they came up for breath. His gaze tangled with hers. Those wild, brilliant blue eyes filled with longing and desire and history and amity. He knew in that second that this time with her had nothing to do with her need to feel liked, or his need to teach her a lesson.

It was about saying goodbye.

He slowly slid her T-shirt over her head, threw it to the couch, then tucked a hand into the hair at her neck as he kissed her long and deep. She held on tight and let him show the way.

The only one with an intimate knowledge of his apartment, Caleb lifted her in his arms and carried her to the stairs.

She leant back and looked into his eyes. Hers were feverish. He told himself it was because she was deep in the throes of passion for him, but even as he thought it he knew it wasn't totally true.

She was a mess. A beautiful mess but a mess all the same. Even if his head felt like cotton wool he doubted hers ever felt that way. There were way too many facts, too many figures, too many memories and worries and ideas rattling around in there for her to ever fully switch them off.

This was not just about sexual gratification for her. It never would be. No matter how much she might hate the fact she was more thoughtful than that. More sensitive.

'Last chance, Doc,' he said, his voice hoarse.

'Caleb,' she said, her voice hoarse and hopeless as she pressed one gentle hand to his cheek. 'Please.'

He didn't need to be asked twice even as he now understood what this was costing her.

He was a cad. He was wicked. He was a selfish bastard.

He was taking advantage of the situation in every possible way. But that was his nature. And it was for the best if she knew it.

He carried her carefully up the skinny winding staircase to his loft bedroom. Once there he let her down, her lean body sliding against his so slowly it was almost unbearable.

She sat back on the bed, bounced a couple of times, then crawled backwards until she was lying on it. Willing, waiting. Her long dark hair splayed across her perfect shoulders. Her chest lifting and falling with each heavy breath. A sexy smile upon her lips. The brightest of internal lights in her eyes.

He got down on his knees at the foot of the bed and grabbed her feet. Her brow furrowed. Not what she was expecting? Good.

He ran his thumbs up her insteps and her head lolled back, eyes closed, mouth open. 'Oh, God, yes, more of exactly that, please,' she said.

He grinned and did as he was told. Just long enough for her to fall into a state of complete relaxation. Then he wrapped his hands around her feet and tugged. Her elbows slid out from beneath her and she landed flat on her back with a bounce.

Her breath whooshed out of her lungs in a great squeal of surprise. Followed by a peal of laughter. 'That was just cruel,' she said.

'Ava, my sweet, you haven't yet seen how cruel I can be.'

He took one foot, covered it in his warm hands and blew hot air along her sole. He half expected her to feign indifference, to hold back, it was what he would have done, but her hands gripped mounds of blanket and she arched away from him. When she came down it seemed she couldn't get enough air.

Her susceptibility to his every touch shouldn't have surprised him. Not after the times he'd been with her. But here, now, this time everything felt strangely heightened. He actually wondered if she might come before he'd even moved higher than her foot.

He clasped a hand around her ankle and tugged. She slid further down the bed, her hair splaying out beneath her head like a fan of dark silk. He ran a hand beneath her jeans, and up her calf. Only then did he remember her jeans were knee-deep in dry mud.

'What on earth were you doing before you came here?' he growled.

She opened her eyes, lifted her head and glanced at her jeans, then grinned. 'Wouldn't you like to know?'

'What I'd like is to not get mud all over my clean bed sheets.'

She moved up onto her elbows again and looked him right in the eye as she said, 'If you want me to take my jeans off, Caleb, you only have to ask.'

'Where have you been all my life?' he asked.

She laughed. Her laughter sang through him. Soft, pretty, familiar, and much missed. He vowed to collect as much of it as he could before she left.

His stomach clenched.

He ignored it and instead paid close attention as Ava climbed to her knees and slowly, ever so achingly slowly, began to pop the buttons of her fly.

Pop. Pop. Pop.

The top of her panties peeked out from the V of her jeans. He looked again at her bra. It was white cotton and covered in yellow daisies. He looked down. Her panties were pink hipsters with pictures of fairies on them. It took him a moment to realise they didn't match. He wasn't sure he knew that women had it in them to wear mismatched underwear. But Ava, being Ava, wasn't like other women.

It was so ingenuous, so darling, so lacking in ego his hands actually shook. He clenched them into fists at his side so that she wouldn't notice. So that he could pretend it had never happened.

'Ready?' she said, head down, eyes stormy, hair out of control.

God, but she was beautiful. And not just that. She was unique. Never in his life had he known another woman quite like her. And never would he again.

'Ready as I'll ever be,' he said.

She fell onto her back, lifted her legs in the air, yanked her jeans off and hung them from a single finger off the edge of his bed. 'Where do you want 'em? Wouldn't want to dirty your precious floor,' she said.

'Say the word dirty one more time and only you're to blame for what I might do.'

'Dir-r-rty,' she purred.

'Right.' He leapt onto the bed, grabbed the jeans and threw them so far they sailed over the balcony and onto the living-room floor below.

She laughed so hard her knees tucked up to her chest. Her pale knees covered in a smattering of tiny freckles. The muscles beneath his eyes twinged. How could he have forgotten that about her? He kissed one, then the other in reparation.

Then he slowly lowered her legs until she was lying flat. Naked bar her underwear. Looking up at him. Trusting. As though she knew he'd never really hurt her. Where she got that idea he had no idea.

'Hi,' she whispered.

'Hi,' he said.

He leaned down and kissed her. A deep lusty kiss that he'd be perfectly willing to see go on for ever. But he didn't have for ever. He only had tonight. And thus he planned to make every minute count.

He gently caressed her flat tummy with his open palms. She writhed beneath his touch.

He kissed his way up one arm and down the other starting and finishing with the tips of each finger. Her deep sensual breaths punctuated the weighty silence.

He tugged at the peak of her bra until her breast was exposed. She bit her lip, anticipation seeping from every pore. Then he took her nipple in his mouth, suckling until he thought he might be the one to fall apart with the best still yet to come.

She tucked a leg around his back, found he was still wearing the towel and whipped it off with her toes.

'So that's what they teach you at those fancy schools.' He kissed his way back up to the edge of her lips and wondered then how he'd been able to stay away from that heavenly mouth for so long.

He felt her smile against his mouth. 'And that's just in orientation.'

He slowly circled her belly button with the tip of a finger. 'Did they teach you this?' he whispered between kisses.

'First year,' she said on a release of breath as her eyes fluttered closed.

He let his fingers trail slowly down her belly, until they tickled her soft dark hair. 'How about this?'

'Wait,' she said, her voice ragged, 'hang on. Yep. Uh-huh. That was for extra credit.'

'Then how about this?' His fingers didn't move. Yet her whole body tensed in expectation of what was to come. He slowed his kisses until their lips barely touched. It was sweet agony. And for a guy who never denied himself anything it was a revelation.

Then he cupped her, stroked her, and she was rendered speechless. Her right knee fell sideways as she opened herself up to him and he let himself marvel at the woman she had become.

He found himself wanting to prolong everything. To take as long as she'd let him to please her. And only after she fell apart and long after her trembling ceased did he find a condom in his bedside drawer, slide it into place and lever himself above her.

He waited for her to open her eyes so that she could see who it was who could break her down as he had. She looked deep into his eyes and she smiled. Her lovely, sweet, sexy, debilitating smile.

Ava...

This time her name came to him in his own voice. Deep, croaky and wretched.

He sank inside her, a perfect fit. She wrapped her legs about him, ran her fingers through his hair and moved with him as though they were listening to the exact same beat in their heads.

She clung to him, her fingers biting into his shoulders, her sweat intermingling with his.

Eons later she released his name on a long forlorn sigh. And just as he felt the sweet tension peaking inside him she tumbled into bliss in his arms. And he in hers.

They fell back to earth together, holding one another close, their breaths easing slowly, slowly.

She continued to press herself against him as closely as she possibly could. It felt as though she was trying to get under his skin.

If only she knew she had been there all along.

CHAPTER TWELVE

Ava stood out on Caleb's balcony, wearing an oversized T-shirt of his she'd found hanging over a chair in his room. And nothing else bar the leather strap and locket he'd bought her for her sixteenth birthday.

The locket which to this day still had his picture inside.

As she blinked up into the dusty night sky her limbs were warm, her mind racing. But for the first time in as long as she could remember her heart felt settled.

She loved Caleb. Had done as long as she'd known him. There was no other man for her out there in the big wide world. She'd looked. She'd sampled and she'd only been disappointed again and again.

Because the only place she needed to have looked was in her own backyard. It was so obvious to her now she couldn't even imagine the mental roadblocks she must have steadfastly kept in place all these years so as not to see it.

The light spring breeze tickled the bare skin at the edges of the T-shirt.

Could it ever be possible that the reason he'd been such hard work this weekend was because he might in fact love her, too? And had all this time?

She shivered and wrapped her arms about herself, wanting to feel the lingering heat of his touch as long as she could.

The swoosh of the sliding door told her she was no longer alone. A satisfied smile stretched across her face as Caleb slid behind her, tucking his length along hers, and nibbling the soft spot below one ear.

'Have you ever seen such stars?' she asked.

'You asked me that last night. You need some new material.'

'Well, they're worth a second mention.'

Caleb's nuzzling stopped for as long as it took for him to look up, then he was back at it again, creating wave upon wave of goose bumps over every inch of exposed skin. 'Don't get the appeal myself,' he said. 'Then again I'm not in the least bit romantic. As far as I'm concerned stars are stars.'

She shrugged into Caleb's T-shirt, the scent of him corrupting her every which way. 'You forget I haven't seen these exact stars in a very long time. See there, low in the east Pisces, the fish, and Cetus, the whale. Mira, a star within Cetus periodically changes its brightness.'

This time when Caleb stopped nuzzling, he wrapped his arms about her waist and looked up, tucking her head beneath his chin. Her lungs squeezed tight with pure happiness.

'Don't tell me you studied astronomy too.'

'Only enough basic concepts of astronomy and astrophysics to pass the Harvard post-grad written placement examination. But by then I realised how much applied maths and how little star-gazing would be involved in the post-grad studies, so I let it go.'

'Mmm, all work and no play. Doesn't sound like my cup of tea, either.'

'Big shock.'

'So,' he said, 'tell me what's so special about these stars that has kept you away from my bed for far too long.'

She slid her arms along the top of his, the rasp of masculine hair creating a whole new level of shivers within her. 'These stars are special because they only look like this in this part of the world. Looking up at the Milky Way, arching across the sky from north-east to south-west, I know I'm home. See?'

'Nothing I didn't learn at the school trip to the Brisbane Planetarium so far, Ms Ivy League. I'd ask for my money back if I was you.'

'Fine. Then look directly overhead and you'll see Capricornus, the sea-goat, and Aquarius, the water carrier.'

She held up her arm and pointed, leaning back into him so that he could have the best view. His hand found her elbow and slunk along her arm until it was wrapped around her hand. She leaned back even further, his warmth became her warmth and the stars almost became irrelevant. Almost.

Knowledge had been the one thing that had helped her make sense of the crazy, chaotic, confusing world around her, and now she just loved imparting everything she'd learned to others. Having a doctorate under her belt would bring her place in academia to an end, releasing her out into the big wide world to share what she knew with kids just like her.

The thought of her doctorate, of Harvard, of the review committee, and of leaving this place, lassoed her freed spirit and brought it back down to earth.

She leant deeper into Caleb's sinew and strength, allowing his indomitable strength to cushion her.

'And over there,' she said, 'towards the south-west there's the Southern Cross. It can't be seen from the northern hemisphere yet its visible here throughout the entire year. It never disappears below the horizon. Isn't that something?'

'It's gorgeous.'

'It's constant is what it is. Standing anywhere in this city, on any given night, looking skyward, and seeing those five stars is about the only thing I've ever been able to truly count on.'

Caleb's grip abated, just a tad. But just enough.

She let her arm drop. Suddenly the cool of the night enveloped her, winding itself around her even though to all intents and purposes she was still in Caleb's arms.

But she no longer felt as though she was in his embrace.

'We can do this, right?' she whispered.

'Do what?' he asked, sliding a hand beneath her T-shirt to trace his fingers along her naked ribs.

It felt decadent, it felt delicious, and she knew he was trying to distract her. It was working.

But out there on his balcony, staring at the wide Australian sky, her train of thought had been important. Imperative. The next five minutes might well decide the course of her life.

'Stop, Caleb, I can't think when you do that.'

'So stop thinking.' He replaced his fingers with the palm of his hand, making gentle yet insistent tracks across her belly. It flinched agonisingly under every small caress.

She turned in his arms to find he was shirtless. All hard, tanned muscle gleaming in the moonlight. Blue and white striped pyjama pants hanging low off his hips. And by the feel of him he wore nothing underneath.

He was gorgeous. Just far too gorgeous and charismatic and provocative for it to be in any way fair. 'Caleb…'

His answering smile was flirtatious. Deliberately so. 'Yes, Ava?'

'I'm going back to Harvard.'

His eyes grew dark, and not from desire. 'Of course you are.'

She bit her lip. That wasn't the response she'd been hoping for. Neither had she expected him to get down on his knees and beg her to stay. Something in between would have been helpful. So she explained herself further to make sure he really heard her.

'Going back won't be pretty. In fact, it's going to get pretty ugly. But a lot of people have put a lot of faith in me over the years. The scholarships alone have saved me hundreds of thousands in student debt. I owe the companies and organisations who've sponsored me to finish what I started. To be all they thought I could be.'

'Ava, honey,' he said. 'You're going to have to let go this desperate need of yours to be liked or you'll for ever be turning in circles trying to please everybody but yourself.'

'You're right,' she said. 'I know you're right. This weekend has shown me the time has come to do what I have to do to please myself as nobody else is going to do it for me. Of all the schools I've been to Harvard really fits. It's one of the finest schools in the world and I'd be a fool to give up everything I've worked so hard for.'

The fact was, when all was said and done, she was her parents' child. She was a Halliburton. It was in her blood not to accept less than everything she'd ever wanted.

She wanted to finish out her schooling at Harvard.

She wanted to ace her doctorate.

And she wanted Caleb.

'I guess what I'm asking,' she said, 'is if you'll wait for me.'

He didn't move. Didn't flinch. He didn't even blink. He just looked at her with those dark shadowed eyes. And suddenly she felt very cold.

'I have a year left on my dissertation. And then I could teach, or speak, or consult anywhere in the world. I could come home for good. But with the right incentive I'd do everything in my power to finish sooner.'

Eventually the muscles in his jaw worked as he squinted

off into the distance. 'It must help having such sway on the panel,' he said. 'Well done there.'

'Such sway?' *No. He did not just say that.* Her voice was reed-thin as she said, 'Caleb, that's over. I see now that it was over before it even began. You have to believe me.'

She reached a hand up to his cheek and he jerked away. Her hand closed in on itself as though burned.

He wasn't really being as mean as he was trying to be. He was protecting himself. She knew him well enough to know that his bravado was a shell. Beneath his slick surface was the most genuine, deep, tender man she'd ever known. That man was the man she loved.

Her next words clogged in her throat. But if this blistering affair was ever to become anything more they had to be said.

Trying not to feel as if this was her last chance to get this right, she took a deep breath and said, 'But you've already waited all this time.'

After several long seconds, he stepped away from her, distancing himself physically and emotionally. It left her shaking, and wishing she'd thought to put on a robe.

'You said it yourself,' he said. 'The opportunities over there are unmatched. Why come back at all?'

She rubbed a hand across her forehead, which suddenly felt abnormally tight. 'Well, for you. For us. For this. Caleb—'

'I don't do stale pizza,' he said. 'I don't do sleepovers. I don't do commitment. I do five-star luxury all the way. Blithe self-indulgence. Absolute independence. Are you saying you're sophisticated enough to handle that?'

His words made no sense. Not after the way he looked at her, and treated her, and the way she felt when she was with him. The way the first place she'd wanted to run when she'd felt backed into a corner was not as far away as possible but into his arms. And not after the way he'd taken her in.

Had she been the one to read everything the wrong way? Heck, she'd done it enough times in every other relationship she'd ever forged—why should her relationship with Caleb be any different? Could she truly be the world's greatest fool?

She grabbed a tight hold of the freezing cold metal railing and glared at the stars that twinkled back at her: pretty and completely unhelpful.

'Why?' she asked them, the hot sting of humiliation burning the backs of her eyes. 'Why is it that I always get the same response?'

At the hitch in her voice, she felt Caleb finally stir.

She turned on him with a vengeance. 'Don't you dare look at me like that.'

'Like what?'

'Like I'm some poor washed-up kitten in need of coddling. I'm not a kid, Caleb. I'm a grown woman. I'm smart, I'm not cross-eyed, I can hold a conversation, I can cook a mean pot roast, mothers always seem to like me.'

Ava felt her breaths coming more shallow and more frequently. But now she'd started she couldn't stop. After she'd given herself to Caleb the way she had, and received so much more of him than she'd ever thought possible, her emotions had become a runaway train.

She looked deep into his eyes and asked the one thing, despite all her schooling, that she'd never been able to figure out:

'What makes me so hard to love?'

A-w-w w, hell, Caleb thought, his throat constricting to the point of physical pain.

What had begun as a night of sexual fireworks, of passion reignited, of fantasies lived out, of the most sublime, free, spontaneous release of his young life, had suddenly spun on a dime and become very very real.

He was a proud man, a strong man, a man who was used to having things fall his way. But the time had come to admit the memory of the day he'd asked her to stay for him and she'd walked away had scarred him deep. And he never wanted to feel that diminished, that fallible, that way ever again.

'Honey,' he said, the words feeling like acid on his tongue, 'I'm not the one to ask.'

'Why not you?' she asked, her big blue eyes shimmering, wounded.

He dug his toes hard into the tiles until they hurt. 'Because I'm not the till-death-do-us-part, happy-family-guy type. I can't do long distance. Hell, I'm not even all that good at short-distance relationships. I'm not the one you want.'

'So you're telling me that you don't want me. After what just happened in there, and everything else that went on between us this weekend, you are standing there and telling me that it was all just sex.'

'Maybe I am.'

'Maybe?' Her eyes were so full of hope. But it wasn't the hope of someone looking forward to a bright rosy future. It was the hope of someone clinging to a life raft.

'Honey, there's no maybe about it. I told you I'm no good at being nice. I'm rotten to the core.'

To prove it he dragged her to him and kissed her. It was intense, stupefying, consuming.

She melted in his arms, clinging to him, kissing him with such unchecked ardour that for the first time in his entire privileged life he wished he were a different kind of guy. And it was all her fault.

The kiss suddenly tasted of salt. He pulled away. Wiped his thumb across his lips and came away with her tears.

All he could do was stare as her bright blue eyes became great wells of sadness. The fact that it was his fault, his Ava, made him feel as if he'd just entered the seventh level of hell.

'Ava…'

She held up a hand while she collected herself. Her voice was ragged, and so tired when she said, 'Damien and Chelsea are going on their honeymoon tomorrow. Perhaps I should take that as a sign I ought to go back then too.'

She glanced at him, for a few long seconds, giving him one more chance to be a man and take up her tender-hearted request that he be the one to love her as no one had ever loved her.

He might well have been stubborn and selfish, but keeping her dangling for his own ends was beneath even him. 'That sounds like a plan,' he said.

Her face crumpled before she looked down at her bare feet. She nodded once, then said, 'Can you do me the favour of staying out here while I collect my things and go? I feel ridiculous enough without having you watch me crawl around on my hands and knees looking for my bra.'

He opened his mouth to ask how she was getting home, but she held up a hand, her eyes dark and smudged and so, so sad he actually found breathing a struggle.

'If you ask me if I need cab money I will push you off the balcony.'

He shut his mouth. And smiled as he was meant to do.

She smiled back, or at least tried her very best.

Then she leaned in and kissed him on the cheek. Orange blossoms mixed with his cologne to form the sweetest scent he'd ever known.

'Goodbye, Caleb,' she said. Then her hand slid from his chest and she was gone.

He stayed out on that balcony for a long time after she closed his front door. Staring at the stars. Wondering what a sky without the Southern Cross would look like. He'd never paid attention when he'd had the chance to before.

He decided the thought of looking skyward and not recognising a thing was the reason he suddenly felt as if something were missing inside him.

CHAPTER THIRTEEN

MONDAY morning Caleb sat in his spacious corner office at Keppler, Jones and Morgenstern, the crack day-trading sensation he had run alongside Damien for the past six years.

His right knee jiggled in rhythm with the pen he tapped against the leather pad atop his desk and he stared blankly at the tropical fish populating the screensaver on his computer screen.

The markets had been open for over an hour. He had a dozen leads on new mid-level clients looking for representation. And he had yet to pick up the phone.

It was all Ava Halliburton's fault.

When she'd left the first time he'd cut her from his life cold turkey. This time, while he should have been ambivalent at best, he found he didn't like the idea one little bit.

For the time he'd spent with her over the past thirty-six hours made him feel like a super-fast train hitting a coin on the tracks. Everything he was once so content with in his life was becoming steadily and rapidly unstuck.

A sound had him glancing up to find Damien lounging in the doorway, relaxed and cool in jeans and a black cashmere jumper.

'Jeez, you startled me, mate.' Caleb let his bouncy office

chair tilt forward and took to shuffling random papers on his desk. 'Aren't you on your honeymoon yet? What the hell's wrong with you?'

Damien grinned. 'This afternoon we head off. Two weeks on the beach in Antigua. Just me, the wife, a kilometre of pure white sand, a hammock, margaritas on tap, the wife—'

'You can't imagine how happy I am for you.'

Damien's grin only widened. 'So are you really happy to run the place on your own while I'm away?'

Caleb leaned back in his chair and feigned ambivalence. 'Mmm. Happy? Happy's a strong word. And I did just download Space Invaders and I was hoping to spend the next fortnight beating my top score from when I was sixteen…'

'Shouldn't be hard. You always sucked at Space Invaders.'

'Says the man who looks at anything silver with buttons and lights and calls for help. But worry not, my friend, when you return I will hand the puppet-master strings back to you. Too much admin and not enough schmoozing for me. If that's why you're here.'

Damien pushed away from the door and sauntered over to the window, hands clasped behind his back, shoulders straight. 'It's not.'

'No, I didn't think so.'

'I tried to call you last night and couldn't get a hold of you.'

Caleb let the silence swell, knowing Damien's temperament meant he'd be more likely to bend to fill it. While he himself was stubborn enough to keep his lips buttoned for a lifetime if need be. He'd proven that well enough.

He ran a hand hard across the back of his neck, a move he'd perfected since Ava had come back to town. He let his hand drop.

'So is that where you were?' Damien asked. 'Schmoozing new clients?'

'Nope.'

'Trawling the seedier parts of Melbourne for a new place in which to schmooze clients?'

'Nuh-uh.'

Just ask me, buddy, he thought. *At least give me that much credit.*

This conversation had been six months in the coming, ever since he'd stupidly opened his big mouth and told Damien how he'd once felt about his sister. Hell, it had been coming from the day they'd first met.

Caleb and his family had just moved into Stonnington Drive during his last year of high school and he'd been dragged along to play golf with his father, Damien's father and Damien. The neither of them had much taken to the other: two teenage bulls locking horns.

Until Ava with her long dark hair in plaits, glasses perched atop her small nose, mouth in a tight line, had stormed out from the cluster of willow trees to the side of the fifth hole, jeans knee-deep in mud, bright blue eyes fierce enough to cow a grown man.

She'd ramped up to Damien, kicked him in the shin, called him something that in the eyes of a fourteen-year-old had no doubt seemed the worst she could come up with, glared at Caleb for being in her brother's general vicinity, then stormed off.

Ralph Halliburton had laughed uproariously, Damien had blushed, and Caleb, empathetic soul he had been at that age, had felt sorry for the guy and patted him on the back. The two of them had forged the tightest of friendships then and there.

Funny, he'd never asked what had made Ava so angry that day. He looked to Damien, the words tickling the tip of his tongue, then he realised this was not the time.

Damien was no longer looking out the window, he was staring at Caleb.

If Caleb was in any way honest with himself, which he tried his very best not to be much of the time, he'd been a little smitten with his best friend's sister from that very moment.

He'd never met such a tough, feisty or fantastic woman. To this very day…

Caleb pushed his chair back and stood. Eye to eye with his business partner. 'Come on, Damo,' he said, 'spit it out. I haven't got all day.'

'Fine. Were you with Ava last night?'

Caleb's bristling neck hairs felt so on end they were likely horizontal. 'Some of the time, yes.'

Damien's cheek twitched. Caleb looked from one eye to the other trying to decipher if his friend was preparing himself to throttle him or to welcome him to the family.

Caleb had no intention of laying down to the first. And as to the second… A Halliburton. With Ava. Til death do they part. The indecipherable empty space that had appeared in his chest the night before squeezed a size smaller.

'Are you really prepared to ask what we were up to?' he asked.

'Not likely. Though I am prepared to ask what your intentions are regarding my sister.'

Caleb laughed, though the sound hurt the back of his throat. 'You're kidding, right?'

Damien's usually friendly face gave nothing away. 'I'm not kidding,' he said. 'You are you, after all.'

Caleb stood taller, hoping this wouldn't turn any more difficult than it was. Damien was his partner in a multimillion-dollar business, but he was also his best mate.

Would it all come down to this?

And why was telling Damien that he had no intentions so hard?

'Meaning?' he asked.

'Come on, buddy. This is me you're talking to. I know your history with women. It might be enviable but it ain't pretty.'

Caleb had no words. Because Damien was spot on. He was never hard up for a date. Yet, of all the desirable segments of his life, on that front alone he was a restless man.

'She's been through a lot,' Damien said.

'So I gather.'

'I'm not mucking about here. I've seen enough tears from that girl to never want to see her cry again. And if that means I have to stick my nose where it's not wanted in order to ensure her happiness, or at the very least to ensure she's not unduly unhappy, I will.'

Caleb knew Damien was doing what he had to do: protect his sister from the big bad wolf. But what he hadn't realised until that moment was how completely he wanted to protect her, too.

He didn't want to see her hurt. Especially by him.

He didn't want to see her run. Especially from him.

He loved the woman far too much to let anything stand in the way of her getting *everything* she ever wanted.

He loved her?

By Jove, he loved her. He, Caleb Gilchrist, the shark of Collins Street, the last of the confirmed bachelors, was in love.

Well, what do you know? That explained a hell of a lot. The fact that he'd never allowed another woman to get too close. The fact that sleeping with Ava had been more intense, more spectacular, more…everything than with anyone else. It explained the sense of a great gaping hole in his chest the moment she'd left. The ensuing fuzz in his head where his brain had once been. It was the only explanation why he'd been silly enough to be with her again despite the fact that she'd left him once before.

He let his head sink into his hands. If only he'd figured that out twelve hours beforehand. Then maybe she wouldn't be out there in the world feeling as bewildered as he was.

'I don't want to see her hurt any more than you do,' he muttered through his fingers as he ran them over his face.

When he peeked at Damien the guy seemed royally unconvinced.

He could have told him what he now knew, but some latent sense of honour made it impossible to tell anyone how he felt about her before he was able to tell her.

Caleb swallowed down the lump in his throat, looked his best friend in the eye and said, 'My relationship with Ava is between the two of us. Always has been, always will be.'

Damien watched him closely for several long seconds before his shoulders relaxed, then he reached over and took Caleb in his arms, giving him two manly slaps on the back. 'You know what: I think that's the best answer you could have given me. Best of luck there, buddy. She's a livewire. I don't envy you your future one little bit.'

'Right,' Caleb said, not quite sure what to do bar slap his friend back. 'Thanks.'

After one last extra-hard slap that Caleb thought was a bit past the edge of friendly, Damien let go.

'Will you be here when I get back?' Damien asked.

And while three days earlier that might have been the most ridiculous question he'd ever been asked, Caleb found himself floundering for an answer.

When Caleb said nothing, Damien nodded as though that was the right thing to have said, or not said, as well.

'Well, I'm off,' Damien said. 'Ava's flight leaves only a couple of hours after ours. But you knew that, right?'

Caleb, feeling completely and utterly out of his depth,

another new experience to add to the many he was enduring that day, still said nothing.

Damien laughed, gave him one last pat on the arm, then was gone.

Ava stood on the back terrace of her family home, staring out across the pristine garden, past the conifers to the golf course beyond the creek.

Beyond that was the city of Melbourne and somewhere in the middle of the hustle and bustle, wheeling and dealing and making more money than any one human could ever possibly require, was Caleb.

She felt as if she were coming down with the flu, but she knew better. Her body still ached for him. Ached because of him. She had come down with love for a man who didn't love her back. Or at least didn't love her enough.

It was the story of her life.

She glanced at her watch. Fifteen minutes before Damien and Chelsea would have to leave if they didn't want to miss their plane.

Her bags were packed and she had her passport and her airline ticket in the back pocket of her jeans. And while the last time she'd gone she'd felt almost giddy with the pleasure of cutting every string capable of holding her back, this time she felt herself wanting to cling to the strings so tight she was desperately afraid they might snap for good.

Because the last time she had been a little kid running away from home. From a place where she'd felt she didn't belong. And finally from the very adult knowledge that she already cared for Caleb deeply enough that she would change for him, then one day, when it all crumbled and fell apart, as her parents' supposedly solid marriage had done, she would crumble and fall apart with it.

This time she was twenty-nine. Her range of experience was far greater. Now she knew more about risk and reward, about joy and regret, and even about the many different kinds of love. She now understood that most people found it so difficult to show love for fear they might not get it in return.

At one time the whole Halliburton family could have been poster children for keeping their hearts dark and private places. Herself included. But now…

Damien was married.

Her parents had reconciled.

And the night before, in Caleb's arms, she had realised that the reason she had kept the splendour of her heart a tightly closed secret was that there was only one man on earth who already held the key.

She wouldn't take back a second of the journey that had led her to that revelation; in the end it would be her salvation, but, boy, did the growing pains hurt.

'Ava?'

She took in a shaky breath as she turned. 'Hey, Dad.'

He moved to stand beside her, no coffee, and no newspaper to hide behind. 'You're heading off today, I hear.'

'Any minute now.'

He nodded. 'When you didn't come home last night I…' He stopped. Swallowed. 'I was hoping that this time you wouldn't see the need to leave without saying goodbye. No matter how much I had it coming. Then and now.'

'Dad, it's okay—'

'No,' he said, holding a hand in front of him. 'It's not. You didn't deserve my censure. Not you. Not ever. You've always been a good girl. My sweet girl.'

Ava ducked her head so that he wouldn't see that her cheeks were beginning to tremble. 'Dad—'

He kept his gaze dead ahead. 'I always loved this house.

I thought it was the kind of place a man couldn't help but raise a happy family.'

'Are *you* happy?' she asked.

He finally glanced her way, surprise etched across his handsome face.

'I know there was a long time there that you weren't,' she said. 'But now? Are you and Mum both happy?'

His face softened. Melted. And Ava saw in him what Caleb had seen the other night. Love.

Clever Caleb. Sensitive Caleb. Tender Caleb. If only he had a clue that he wasn't the granite-hearted hedonist he did his very best to be. If only...

Her father said, 'You know your mother—so long as she has access to a tennis court and a blender she does not know how not to be happy. But as for me, I can only truly be happy if I know that you and your brother are both happy.'

She smiled. There was no way she was going to burden him with all the ways she knew she could be happier. This was more than the two of them had said to one another in years and it felt so precious she didn't want to do a thing to ruin it.

'Ava!' Damien called out from deep within the house. 'Move it or lose it!'

She took a deep breath of Melbourne air. 'Time to hit the road. Thanks for letting me stay, Dad. I'm really glad I came home.'

His chest puffed out, chin up, warmth hidden behind his usual strong façade. 'Just don't be gone so long next time, you hear?'

She leant her head on his shoulder for just a moment and he let her. 'I love you too, Dad.'

'Ava!'

She lifted her head and screamed, 'Coming, Damien! Jeez.'

Her father followed her into the house and carried her suitcase to the front door. 'Come back soon.'

'I'll try.'

'I mean it. I'll need saving from your mother's intervention once you're gone. And from Damien's holiday snaps. And Caleb's sulking. Oh, Lord, I'd forgotten about Caleb's sulking. Last time you left it must have been a good year before he cracked a ribald joke again. You really have always been his favourite.'

She gave her dad a quick kiss on the cheek, knowing too much too soon and the poor man would likely expire from the indelicacy of it. And knowing there was no way she could make a ribald joke herself under the circumstances.

Then she grabbed her suitcase and headed out into the bright spring day, letting the overbright midday sun do its dandiest to burn away the image she couldn't seem to shake from her mind.

Caleb, standing half naked on his balcony. Moonlight silhouetting his beautiful body against the stunning city skyline. His shadowed eyes giving nothing away as she offered him her heart.

The only man for her.

But not her man.

Caleb glanced at the clock on the wall.

It was just after midday. Ava would be heading to the airport right that minute. Likely in the back of some smelly cab in which the driver would have decided to take her the long route the second he saw that sweet mug coming out of that big house.

'Sir?'

He looked around the oval conference table at his team, who all had mugs of steaming hot coffee in their hands, and looks of faint concern in their eyes that their intrepid make-shift leader obviously wasn't firing on all cylinders.

But he was deep in thought. Important thought. Out-rageous, putting-an-end-to-the-easy-life-as-he-knew it type thoughts.

He was a big fish in a small pond. He was infamous for getting the ungettable gets. He was feared by other firms and adored by their clients. He had a swanky apartment with a knockout city view, he was known by name at all of the top clubs in town, and his little black book was peopled with the kinds of women men of his ilk would kill for.

Yet Caleb was sitting there at his one-of-a-kind conference table looking out over his million-dollar view contemplating throwing it all away. And for what?

For her, that was what.

She had run once before and, being that he'd been a novice in the ways of love, he'd simply let her go. Now he was all grown up he knew that kind of connection, and history, and friendship, and *égalité* in any relationship was rare. It was more than rare; it was once-in-a-lifetime stuff. But at least the years had taught him another thing that might be of conse-quence in his current state of upheaval: the only way to get what you wanted was to go out there and get it.

And he wanted Ava. If she was about to run again, then by Jove this time he wasn't going to let her get away.

He scraped his chair back so loud the whole room went quiet.

'Mindy,' Caleb said, waggling a finger at Damien's execu-tive assistant, a tall, strong-featured, diligent sort of woman Caleb had always thought very able, when he'd thought of her at all, 'you can take over from here, right? Run the joint for a bit?'

'How long's a bit?'

'Your guess is as good as mine.'

Her mouth hung open for a brief second before her shoulders squared, her eyes narrowed and she nodded. 'Of course I can.'

'Good for you, Mindy.'

Caleb rounded the table, kissed her atop her curly head, gave a big wave to the Keppler, Jones and Morgenstern crew who must have thought he'd caught the bug that had turned Damien from a cool, sharp, focused boss into a man who took half-days three times a week.

And they were right.

He jogged down the hallway, stopping only to grab his car keys.

Only once he and Mae West were stopped in traffic did he hope against hope that her cab driver was taking Ava on a really, really long route to the airport.

Because he had a couple of quick stops to make before he got there.

CHAPTER FOURTEEN

AND that was how Caleb found himself at the airport on a mission to stop Ava from leaving. Again. He refused to let the overwhelming sense of déjà vu temper his mood.

To his left ceiling-to-floor windows showed the coming and going of countless multicoloured planes. To his right a stream of interchangeable fast-food outlets was a blur on the edge of his vision. And all around him people were either meeting or leaving loved ones.

He felt the heightened emotions running through the place like a terrier nipping at his heels. But for all that he didn't have time to empathise, or the inclination to wonder if it was all that manly to do so. All he could do was use every instinct in his arsenal to reach out and find Ava.

Because this time was different. Because the three things burning holes in the pockets of his suit jacket *made* this time different. As did the years lived, the things realised and admitted, at least to himself. And the way he felt in his heart.

Ava…

The only woman who'd ever really seen him as more than a good time or a road to the good life. The only woman he'd ever let close enough to see beneath the playboy façade he'd spent a lifetime protecting. The only woman for him.

He ducked sideways so as not to run smack bang into a wall of boys in matching team tracksuits. Once through, he headed towards the international food court at a jog.

He, Caleb Gilchrist, the shark of Collins Street, the man least likely to let fancies run away with his cool heart, was running through the Melbourne Airport terminal with his heart well and truly on his sleeve.

'Caleb?'

His name called in that voice brought him to a screeching halt so fast he skidded into a pile of luggage balanced precariously high on a trolley. He banged his shin, hopped on one foot and watched in slow motion as the luggage toppled to the floor.

He glanced over his shoulder, looking for Ava. It had been her voice. It had been his name. Unless he was so far gone he'd been imagining it.

'Oh, dear.'

He looked back to find the owner of the luggage was an older woman not much taller than half his height. What could he do but smile through his teeth and repack her ridiculous amount of baggage? Seriously, where could the woman be going to need that much luggage in this day and age—?

'Caleb?'

He turned to find Ava weaving her way through a row of seats, sliding a dog-eared novel into her leather backpack, glasses on the tip of her nose that was suspiciously pink.

His poor, newly unfettered heart clunked mercilessly against his ribs. He and his damn pride had made her cry. If his shin wasn't already pooling with blood where it had met with what must have been a bowling ball inside one of the lady's bags he would have kicked himself until it hurt just as much.

'What are you doing here?' Ava asked.

'Dear, do you mind...?' the old lady said, looking as helpless as an old lady with skis, and a guitar case, and a tent bag on her pile of luggage could.

He held a hand out to Ava. 'Give me a second.'

She nodded. Caleb tossed the luggage back up onto the trolley. When he bent down to pick up one of the more awkward ones, shaped something like a harp, Ava grabbed the other end.

'Thanks,' he said over the top of the bag as his eyes roved over every glorious underdressed inch of her that he'd half feared he'd never see again.

'Any time,' she said, seemingly unable to take her eyes off him either.

Once the lady was packed and trundling towards the exit Caleb brushed his suddenly damp palms down his suit trousers and drank his fill of Ava.

Hair pinned up into a messy pony tail, denim jacket with a red hoodie underneath, beige cords slouching off her fine frame, flat red leather shoes that looked as if they'd been pre-owned a dozen times over.

And that face. That pale skin, those apple cheeks, those dazzling blue eyes, that wide mouth. That beautiful, familiar, lovable face...

The urge to just take her in his arms and kiss her sense-less, and touch her all over, and make love to her until they fell asleep in one another's arms, was almost overwhelming. How he'd thought he could ever let her go again he had no idea.

'Hi,' he said.

'Hi,' she said, her voice breathy. Unsure. And no wonder after the way he'd behaved. 'What are you doing here?'

This was it. His moment to convince her he'd been a fool, but now he was ready to admit that at least he was her fool. Never in his entire life had he felt so nervous.

He took a deep breath and reached into his pocket, wrapped his hand around the enabler within. 'Thought you might need this.'

He held her white daisy bra from one finger.

Ava stared at it for a few seconds before she realised what it was. She snatched it out of his hand. 'I looked everywhere last night. Where did you find it?'

'It was sticking out from under my couch downstairs. If my memory serves, you were in some kind of hurry to get rid of it last night.'

Ava held up her hand, realised it was the one holding the bra, then slapped it back down beside her. 'I was there. I don't require a play by play. It didn't occur to you that you could post it to me?'

'I don't have your address.'

'Ah, Damien might. Or my parents.'

'Well, silly me, I wasn't thinking of them when I found your bra.'

She hitched her bag higher on her shoulder and gave him nothing. Which was exactly what he deserved. Lucky for him he was an ace at always getting far more than any one man could possibly deserve.

'So,' he said, 'you're really heading back.'

'Yes, I am. I am going back to Harvard, and I'm going to blow the review committee out of the water with my doctoral dissertation. I called Taylor this morning to tell him just that.'

A muscle in Caleb's jaw twitched. If he'd come all this way only to lose her at the last post… He would have no one to blame but himself.

And then she said, 'I asked him to excuse himself from the committee for my doctoral review.'

The words, 'You did not,' shot out of his mouth before he could stop them.

It only made her smile, bringing out the glimmer in those sultry eyes, the adorable apples in those beautiful cheeks. She was so his scruffy beautiful girl it physically hurt to look and not touch.

'I did too,' she said.

'How did he take it?'

'Not well. He seemed to think his partiality would be questioned. And I said that I certainly hoped so. I'm not sure he likes me all that much right now.'

'Fine with me,' Caleb said.

'You know what?' she said. 'It's fine with me, too.'

He got a glimpse of teeth as the smile became a grin. The glimmer of hope that had sent him rushing to be with her was beginning to grow wings.

She blinked up into his eyes, glancing from one to the other as she tried to figure him out as if he were a theory she hadn't quite yet mastered.

Obviously unsuccessful, she bit her lips and looked over her shoulder to the inundation of planes out the window. 'If you came to see Damien and Chelsea off you've missed them.'

'Well, that would have been a great pity if that's why I was here.'

'Oh,' she said. 'It's not?'

'It is, in fact, not.'

They could so small talk like nobody's business. Between them it was practically foreplay, but he'd delayed long enough. Precious seconds were slipping away. Seconds he could be spending with her, not just near her.

He took a deep breath, reached into his left jacket pocket and…

'Young man?'

Caleb frowned and turned to find the old lady with the insane luggage had returned.

'Since you were so kind before I was hoping—'

He held a hand up in front of her face. So kind? Since when did he start to give off good-guy vibes? Just because he was in love, and happy about it—yes, happy, go figure—didn't mean he wasn't still mad, bad and dangerous to know.

'Oh, no, you don't,' he said when she opened her mouth to ask again. 'I'm kind of in the middle of something important here. So, just give me a second.'

Her lips turned down and he actually felt it.

Jeez! He'd brought the triple-threat dream team of the Revolution Wireless owners over to Keppler, Jones and Morgenstern with little more than sweet talk. He could do this.

The lady's pursed lips were soon swept from his mind as he turned back to Ava, his Ava, his sexy, smart, sweet, hopeless, beautiful Ava, took her by the hand and sank to one knee.

The hand still holding her white daisy bra fluttered to her throat. 'Caleb…?'

'Yes, Ava.'

'What are you doing?'

He grinned. 'Sometimes I do wonder what it is they teach you at those fancy schools.'

Ava glanced around at the gathering crowd. 'Caleb, all these people…'

He smiled and waited until her focus was purely on him. Her eyes softened, her shoulders relaxed, and her mouth spread into the beginnings of that glorious wide smile that had chipped away at his heart each and every time he'd seen it in all the years he'd known her.

'No more running,' he said.

'I wasn't, I—' She took a deep breath and let it go.

He nodded. 'Ava. Sweetheart. It's me you're talking to. Me.

Caleb. The boy who riled you, and ribbed you and thought you the cutest, funniest, smartest girl he'd ever known. The young man who knew no better moment than that one beautiful night spent in your arms, but who was too young, too spoilt and too scared to do more than ask you to give up your dreams and stay. The man who thought fast cars and business success and easy living were enough. The man who now realises he would give it all up if you asked him to. The man who won't wait for you because he wants you now. From this day on. For ever.'

As though her legs could no longer hold her upright, she slowly sank down on her knees in front of him. He took her in his arms and hugged her. Just hugged her until she stopped shaking. Then he held her away from him just far enough so he could look into her eyes.

'I know we've been here before,' he said, 'almost in this exact spot, in fact. And I know I screwed everything up last time by not being completely honest about what I wanted, what I needed, and how I felt about you.'

She shook her head as she leaned in and placed a feather-light kiss upon his lips. Sparks exploded behind his eyes before every part of him settled into the most exquisite slow burn.

She said, 'I've never been in this exact place before.'

Tears welled in her big blue eyes. Caleb took in a deep breath lest he join her. Then he pulled a ring box from another inner pocket of his suit jacket.

She took it, opened it, her eyes growing exceedingly wide as she took in the large solitaire. 'Oh, my.'

'Oh, my hurting bank account,' he said.

She laughed her gorgeous laugh and the crowd around them began to cheer, led by the lady with the luggage who was telling them all how the nice man in the suit and tie had helped her earlier.

Caleb stood, helped Ava to her feet, cut through the crowd, looked around for the signs leading to the nearest private lounge and didn't stop until they got there. He tipped the guy at the desk everything in his wallet until he'd secured a couch in a secluded corner.

Ava was still staring at the ring, and he wouldn't have been surprised if she had no idea they'd even moved.

To get her attention back he said, 'Did you know pure gold is so soft it can be moulded by hand?'

She glanced up at him, a slow, steady, sultry smile growing across her face. 'Actually I did.'

'Of course you did. You likely have a degree in molecular chemistry you'd simply forgotten to mention.'

'Only a class or two while I was still at high school.'

She grinned, all bright happy eyes and hope. No wonder he loved her. She got him. And he got her. There was no better feeling.

'Caleb,' she said, then gulped down a lump in her throat. 'Before you say anything else, I want you to know that I have a ticket to return home, booked for three months from now. I planned to achieve the fastest doctorate in the history of the Ivy League so that I could come home and see you and try to convince you that you missed me.'

If Caleb had thought himself skating around the edge of happiness earlier when she'd simply smiled at him, now he knew that was nothing compared with the bloom of feeling invading his every pore at the knowledge she had no intention of letting him go either.

He took the ring box from one hand, the bra from the other, and placed them behind him. For this he wanted her full attention. He reached into the final inner pocket of his suit jacket and pulled out his passport and the printout of confirmation of his plane ticket to Boston that afternoon.

She stared at it. 'But the business…'

'I called Damien from my mobile just before he boarded the plane. He has agreed to buy me out.'

If she'd been surprised to see the ring it was nothing compared with the shock in her eyes. 'But your clients, all the time and money and work you've put into the place—'

'I have the funny feeling rich Americans aren't that different from rich Australians.'

'But—'

'Seriously? Are you trying to talk me out of moving to Boston, opening up a boutique trading firm of my own, and buying an obscenely expensive apartment halfway between the university and the central business district for us to live in? Don't you dare try to talk me out of buying a Cadillac with white-walled tyres and one of those musical horns.'

'You're giving up your whole life. For me?'

He reached out and cupped her cheek. 'I'm taking control of my life. For us. For the longest time I've felt like a big fish in a small pond. And there's nothing I like better than a challenge. And you, my capricious young friend, are the greatest challenge I've ever met. How could I resist?'

He took the ring from the box, held it between his fingers and raised an eyebrow. 'Marry me, Dw.'

Ava nodded, a determined, sure little nod. 'You just try and stop me.'

She leapt into his arms and kissed him. They clung to one another with such intensity he could barely breathe. But breath was overrated compared with what he was getting in return.

When they pulled apart he ran a finger over her cheek, her

chin, her lips. 'Do you have any idea how much I love you Ms Halliburton?'

'If it's even a tenth of the amount I love you, Mr Gilchrist, then I have a pretty good idea.'

He let the ring hover over her hand. 'Even so, I'm not eating stale pizza. Ever.'

She laughed. The sound trickled warmly down his spine.

'Fine,' she said. 'And I'm not ever joining a tennis club.'

Caleb ran a hand over his chin. 'Is that a clincher?'

She slapped him on the arm.

'Whoa. Deal. Anything else I should know about now?' he asked, keeping the ring just out of reach.

Her mischievous face turned serious. 'Even when we drive each other crazy I never want us to end up sleeping in separate bedrooms. Promise me.'

'Honey, if we manage to end up on the same continent then I'm not letting you out of my bed for a week. Separate bedrooms? You'll be lucky to take a separate shower.'

Ava slid her arms around his waist and tucked herself neatly against him, curling her legs over the top of his. 'Is it bad how much I like the sound of that?'

Caleb kissed her on the end of her nose. 'So-o-o bad.'

'Can I have my ring now, please?'

'Are you sure it's not too ostentatious for your liking?'

Her mouth twisted, her cheeks pinked, her eyes devoured the Tiffany setting as if it were the biggest piece of chocolate cake she'd ever seen and she'd just come home after ten years in the desert. 'Nah,' she said. 'It's just ostentatious enough.'

He slipped the ring onto her left ring finger.

It was a perfect fit. It had only taken them fifteen years to realise it.

Caleb shifted Ava until he had access to all the bits of her he planned to get far more up close and personal with the second they found a preposterously sumptuous hotel in Boston.

And he smiled as he leant in to kiss the woman he loved. For he was a happy, happy man.

* * * * *

Tanner heard the rig roll in around sunset. Smiling, he wandered to the window. Watched as Olivia O'Ballivan climbed out of her Suburban, flung one defiant glance toward the house and started for the barn, the golden retriever trotting along behind her.

Taking his coat and hat down from the peg next to the back door, he put them on and went outside. He was used to being alone, even liked it, but keeping company with Doc O'Ballivan, bristly though she sometimes was, would provide a welcome diversion.

He gave her time to reach the horse Butterpie's stall, then walked into the barn.

The golden retriever came to greet him, all wagging tail and melting brown eyes, and he bent to stroke her soft, sturdy back. "Hey, there, dog," he said.

Sure enough, Olivia was in the stall, brushing Butterpie down and talking to her in a soft, soothing voice that touched something private inside Tanner and made him want to turn on one heel and beat it back to the house.

He'd be damned if he'd do it, though.

This was *his* ranch, *his* barn. Well-intentioned as she was, *Olivia* was the trespasser here, not him.

"She's still very upset," Olivia told him, without turning to look at him or slowing down with the brush.

Shiloh, always an easy horse to get along with, stood contentedly in his own stall, munching away on the feed Tanner had given him earlier. Butterpie, he noted, hadn't touched her supper as far as he could tell.

"Do you know anything at all about horses, Mr. Quinn?" Olivia asked.

He leaned against the stall door, the way he had the day before, and grinned. He'd practically been raised on horseback; he and Tessa had grown up on their grandmother's farm in the Texas hill country, after their folks divorced and went their separate ways, both of them too busy to bother with a couple of kids. "A few things," he said. "And I mean to call you Olivia, so you might as well return the favor and address me by my first name."

He watched as she took that in, dealt with it, decided on an approach. He'd have to wait and see what that turned out to be, but he didn't mind. It was a pleasure just watching Olivia O'Ballivan grooming a horse.

"All right, *Tanner*," she said. "This barn is a disgrace. When are you going to have the roof fixed? If it snows again, the hay will get wet and probably mold..."

He chuckled, shifted a little. He'd have a crew out there the following Monday morning to replace the roof and shore up the walls—he'd made the arrangements over a week before—but he felt no particular compunction to explain that. He was enjoying her ire too much; it made her color rise and her hair fly when she turned her head, and the faster breathing made her perfect breasts go up and down in an enticing rhythm. "What makes you so sure I'm a greenhorn?" he asked mildly, still leaning on the gate.

At last she looked straight at him, but she didn't move from

Butterpie's side. "Your hat, your boots—that fancy red truck you drive. I'll bet it's customized."

Tanner grinned. Adjusted his hat. "Are you telling me real cowboys don't drive red trucks?"

"There are lots of trucks around here," she said. "Some of them are red, and some of them are new. And *all* of them are splattered with mud or manure or both."

"Maybe I ought to put in a car wash, then," he teased. "Sounds like there's a market for one. Might be a good investment."

She softened, though not significantly, and spared him a cautious half smile, full of questions she probably wouldn't ask. "There's a good car wash in Indian Rock," she informed him. "People go there. It's only forty miles."

"Oh," he said with just a hint of mockery. "*Only* forty miles. Well, then. Guess I'd better dirty up my truck if I want to be taken seriously in these here parts. Scuff up my boots a bit, too, and maybe stomp on my hat a couple of times."

Her cheeks went a fetching shade of pink. "You are twisting what I said," she told him, brushing Butterpie again, her touch gentle but sure. "I meant…"

Tanner envied that little horse. Wished he had a furry hide, so he'd need brushing, too.

"You *meant* that I'm not a real cowboy," he said. "And you could be right. I've spent a lot of time on construction sites over the last few years, or in meetings where a hat and boots wouldn't be appropriate. Instead of digging out my old gear, once I decided to take this job, I just bought new."

"I bet you don't even *have* any old gear," she challenged, but she was smiling, albeit cautiously, as though she might withdraw into a disapproving frown at any second.

He took off his hat, extended it to her. "Here," he teased. "Rub that around in the muck until it suits you."

She laughed, and the sound—well, it caused a powerful and wholly unexpected shift inside him. Scared the hell out of him and, paradoxically, made him yearn to hear it again.

* * * * *

Discover how this rugged rancher's wanderlust is tamed in time for a merry Christmas, in
A STONE CREEK CHRISTMAS.
In stores December 2008.

Silhouette®

SPECIAL EDITION™

FROM *NEW YORK TIMES* BESTSELLING AUTHOR

LINDA LAEL MILLER

A STONE CREEK CHRISTMAS

Veterinarian Olivia O'Ballivan finds the animals in Stone Creek playing Cupid between her and Tanner Quinn. Even Tanner's daughter, Sophie, is eager to play matchmaker. With everyone conspiring against them and the holiday season fast approaching, Tanner and Olivia may just get everything they want for Christmas after all!

*Available December 2008
wherever books are sold.*

Visit Silhouette Books at www.eHarlequin.com LLMNYTBPA

HARLEQUIN *Presents*

BAD BOY BILLIONAIRES

Ruthless, rebellious and red-hot in bed!

In this brand-new miniseries from Harlequin Presents, these heroes have all that—and a lot more!

The wicked glint in his eye…the rebellious streak that's a mile wide. His untamed unpredictability… The sheer confidence, charisma and barefaced charm of the guy… We can't help but love a bad boy!

Cally usually steers clear of good-looking men— and Blake's off the handsome scale! Blake can see Cally is fiery, so he buys another date with her—this time he'll call the shots….

Available in December

BOUGHT: ONE NIGHT, ONE MARRIAGE
#2785

Virgin Brides, Arrogant Husbands

Demure but defiant...
Can three international playboys
tame their disobedient brides?

Proud, masculine and passionate, these men
are used to having it all. But enter Ophelia,
Abbey and Molly, three feisty virgins to whom
their wealth and power mean little. In stories
filled with drama, desire and secrets of the
past, find out how these arrogant husbands
capture their hearts....

Available in December

THE GREEK TYCOON'S
DISOBEDIENT BRIDE
#2779

REQUEST YOUR FREE BOOKS!

 HARLEQUIN *Presents*®

PASSION GUARANTEED SEDUCTION

2 FREE NOVELS
PLUS 2
FREE GIFTS!

YES! Please send me 2 FREE Harlequin Presents® novels and my 2 FREE gifts (gifts are worth about $10). After receiving them, if I don't wish to receive any more books, I can return the shipping statement marked "cancel". If I don't cancel, I will receive 6 brand-new novels every month and be billed just $4.05 per book in the U.S. or $4.74 per book in Canada, plus 25¢ shipping and handling per book and applicable taxes, if any*. That's a savings of close to 15% off the cover price! I understand that accepting the 2 free books and gifts places me under no obligation to buy anything. I can always return a shipment and cancel at any time. Even if I never buy another book, the two free books and gifts are mine to keep forever.

106 HDN ERRW 306 HDN ERRL

Name _____ (PLEASE PRINT) _____

Address _____ Apt. # _____

City _____ State/Prov. _____ Zip/Postal Code _____

Signature (if under 18, a parent or guardian must sign) _____

Mail to the **Harlequin Reader Service:**
IN U.S.A.: P.O. Box 1867, Buffalo, NY 14240-1867
IN CANADA: P.O. Box 609, Fort Erie, Ontario L2A 5X3

Not valid to current subscribers of Harlequin Presents books.

Want to try two free books from another line?
Call 1-800-873-8635 or visit www.morefreebooks.com.

* Terms and prices subject to change without notice. N.Y. residents add applicable sales tax. Canadian residents will be charged applicable provincial taxes and GST. Offer not valid in Quebec. This offer is limited to one order per household. All orders subject to approval. Credit or debit balances in a customer's account(s) may be offset by any other outstanding balance owed by or to the customer. Please allow 4 to 6 weeks for delivery. Offer available while quantities last.

Your Privacy: Harlequin Books is committed to protecting your privacy. Our Privacy Policy is available online at www.eHarlequin.com or upon request from the Reader Service. From time to time we make our lists of customers available to reputable third parties who may have a product or service of interest to you. If you would prefer we not share your name and address, please check here. ☐

HP08R

HARLEQUIN *Presents*

EXTRA

THE ITALIAN'S BRIDE

Commanded—to be his wife!

Used to the finest food, clothes and women,
these immensely powerful, incredibly
good-looking and undeniably charismatic
men have only one last need: a wife!

They've chosen their bride-to-be and they'll
have her—willing or not!

Enjoy all our fantastic stories in December:

THE ITALIAN BILLIONAIRE'S SECRET LOVE-CHILD
by CATHY WILLIAMS (Book #33)

SICILIAN MILLIONAIRE, BOUGHT BRIDE
by CATHERINE SPENCER (Book #34)

BEDDED AND WEDDED FOR REVENGE
by MELANIE MILBURNE (Book #35)

THE ITALIAN'S UNWILLING WIFE
by KATHRYN ROSS (Book #36)

HPE1208

Coming Next Month

#2779 THE GREEK TYCOON'S DISOBEDIENT BRIDE
Lynne Graham
Virgin Brides, Arrogant Husbands

#2780 THE ITALIAN'S SECRETARY BRIDE Kim Lawrence
Expecting!

#2781 RUTHLESS TYCOON, INNOCENT WIFE Helen Brooks
Ruthless

#2782 THE SHEIKH'S REBELLIOUS MISTRESS
Sandra Marton
The Sheikh Tycoons

#2783 THE MEDITERRANEAN BILLIONAIRE'S BLACKMAIL BARGAIN
Abby Green
Bedded by Blackmail

#2784 BRIDE OF DESIRE Sara Craven
Wedlocked

#2785 BOUGHT: ONE NIGHT, ONE MARRIAGE Natalie Anderson
Bad Boy Billionaires

#2786 HIS MISTRESS, HIS TERMS Trish Wylie
Kept for His Pleasure

Plus, look out for the fabulous new collection
The Italian's Bride, from Harlequin Presents® EXTRA:

#33 THE ITALIAN BILLIONAIRE'S SECRECT LOVE-CHILD
Cathy Williams

#34 SICILIAN MILLIONAIRE, BOUGHT BRIDE
Catherine Spencer

#35 BEDDED AND WEDDED FOR REVENGE
Melanie Milburne

#36 THE ITALIAN'S UNWILLING WIFE
Kathryn Ross